P9-EEK-312

FLIP-iT-OVER
GUIDES TO TEEN EMOTIONS

A Guys' Guide to

Loneliness

Hal Marcovitz

Enslow Publishers, Inc.
40 Industrial Road
Box 398
Berkeley Heights, NJ 07922
USA

http://www.enslow.com

Copyright © 2009 by Enslow Publishers, Inc.

All rights reserved.

No part of this book may be reproduced by any means without the written permission of the publisher.

Library of Congress Cataloging-in-Publication Data

Marcovitz, Hal.
  A guys' guide to loneliness : a girls' guide to loneliness / Hal Marcovitz
and Gail Snyder.
      p. cm. — (Flip-it-over guides to teen emotions)
  Includes bibliographical references and index.
  ISBN-13: 978-0-7660-2856-2 (alk. paper)
  ISBN-10: 0-7660-2856-9 (alk. paper)
  1. Loneliness—Juvenile literature. 2. Girls—Psychology—Juvenile literature. 3.
Boys—Psychology—Juvenile literature. I. Snyder, Gail. II. Title.
  BF575.L7M32 2008
  155.42'424—dc22
                                    2008007666

Printed in the United States of America.

10 9 8 7 6 5 4 3 2 1

Produced by OTTN Publishing, Stockton, N.J.

To Our Readers: We have done our best to make sure all Internet Addresses in this book were active and appropriate when we went to press. However, the author and the publisher have no control over and assume no liability for the material available on those Internet sites or on other Web sites they may link to. Any comments or suggestions can be sent by e-mail to comments@enslow.com or to the address on the title page.

Enslow Publishers, Inc., is committed to printing our books on recycled paper. The paper in every book contains 10% to 30% post-consumer waste (PCW). The cover board on the outside of each book contains 100% PCW. Our goal is to do our part to help young people and the environment too!

Photo Credits: © 2008 Jupiterimages Corporation, 25, 26, 55; Used under license from Shutterstock, Inc., 1, 3, 4, 7, 9, 11, 13, 14, 17, 19, 20, 29, 33, 35, 37, 39, 40, 44, 47, 49, 51, 53, 57.

Cover Photo: Used under license from Shutterstock, Inc.

CONTENTS

CHAPTER ONE

Understanding Loneliness

At his old school, Kyle had always been a good student. He had been on the school's track and soccer teams. And he had always had plenty of friends. But then his father found a new job and the family had to move to a new state.

Kyle didn't know anyone at his new school, and no one seemed interested in him. He didn't try out for the soccer or track teams, because he figured the coaches didn't know him and would cut him anyway. After school, he went straight home and up to his room. He felt lonely and miserable.

Everyone has felt lonely at one time or the other. Feelings of loneliness occur whenever you feel left out, forgotten, unneeded, and ignored. Feeling lonely is more than just being alone (which occurs when a person chooses to be by him- or herself). Loneliness is missing and longing for a connection with other people. Even though Kyle was in the middle of a crowd of kids at school, he felt very lonely because he really didn't know anyone.

Although Kyle was quite good at soccer, he didn't try out for the team because he didn't know anyone.

You and Your Emotions

A part of everyone's personality, emotions are a powerful driving force in life. They are hard to define and understand. But what is known is that emotions—which include anger, fear, love, joy, jealousy, and hate—are a normal part of the human system. They are responses to situations and events that trigger bodily changes, motivating you to take some kind of action.

Some studies show that the brain relies more on emotions than on intellect in learning and in making decisions. Being able to identify and understand the emotions in yourself and in others can help you in your relationships with family, friends, and others throughout your life.

The empty, lost feeling of being lonely can make anyone feel pretty bad. That's why it is often referred to as a negative emotion. Other negative emotions you can experience when lonely include anger, sadness, and grief. You're angry if you think other people aren't being friendly. You're sad because you think you have no friends. You feel grief over having lost old friendships.

Kyle's feelings of loneliness began after the move from his old neighborhood. The stress of being in a new situation affected his behavior. Because Kyle didn't know how to make friends at his new school, he avoided people. He walked to classes alone, and he ate by himself in the school cafeteria. Although he was a good athlete, he didn't try out for the school teams. He didn't want to make an embarrassing mistake in front of kids he didn't know. As he avoided talking

In a telephone survey of approximately a thousand high school students, the Horatio Alger Association found that 16 percent of respondents said a major problem for them was "feeling like no one understands" them. About 11 percent complained of "loneliness or feeling left out" as a major problem.[1]

with other kids, he felt ignored by them. He retreated into his own world and cut off contact with others.

Social loneliness. Kyle was suffering from social loneliness. That is, he no longer had a social group to hang out with. People who have a difficult time making friends typically suffer from social loneliness. And a big reason they have trouble making friends is shyness.

Shyness is that uncomfortable, self-conscious feeling you have when in a new situation or when meeting a stranger. Kyle had never thought of himself as shy before he moved. But he hadn't had much experience dealing with new situations or meeting new people. Now in a new place, he really didn't know what to say or do when he met strangers.

Emotional loneliness. Kyle was also suffering from emotional loneliness. He didn't feel close to anyone. There was no one he felt comfortable with to talk about what was on his mind. He was angry with his parents because of the move, so he didn't want to talk to them either.

With emotional loneliness you don't feel close to anyone—you have no one to share your thoughts and ideas with. You don't think anyone cares about you. And you don't think you can depend on anyone. You can also experience emotional loneliness even when you are part of a social group if you feel like you really can't be open or honest with anyone in that crowd.

Kyle was feeling both social and emotional loneliness because of his family's move. But many other things can affect whether a person feels lonely.

Causes of loneliness. Sometimes you can feel a bit lonely if you come home from school, and no one is around to talk to. You've finished your homework and chores, and you don't have any idea of what to do. Such bored, lonely feelings usually don't last long. They may be easily banished when you

If you find yourself alone and bored, why not catch up on your reading— start a new book or read ahead for some of your classes.

Quiz Yourself

Loneliness can affect physical and mental health.
Because of this, researchers at the University of California Los Angeles have developed the following Revised UCLA Loneliness Scale (RULS) to help health professionals determine whether their patients are lonely.

On a separate piece of paper, take the test. Indicate how often you have felt the way described in each statement, using the following scale:

Scoring for questions in black
4 = I have felt this way often.
3 = I have felt this way sometimes.
2 = I have rarely felt this way.
1 = I have never felt this way.

Scoring for questions in blue
1 = I have felt this way often.
2 = I have felt this way sometimes.
3 = I have rarely felt this way.
4 = I have never felt this way.

1. I feel in tune with the people around me.

2. I lack companionship.

3. There is no one I can turn to.

4. I do not feel alone.

5. I feel part of a group of friends.

6. I have a lot in common with the people around me.

7. I am no longer close to anyone.

8. My interests and ideas are not shared by those around me.

9. I am an outgoing person.

10. There are people I feel close to.

11. I feel left out.

12. My social relationships are superficial.

13. No one really knows me well.

14. I feel isolated from others.

15. I can find companionship when I want it.

16. There are people who really understand me.

17. I am unhappy being so withdrawn.

18. People are around me but not with me.

19. There are people I can talk to.

20. There are people I can turn to.

Health professionals consider a score of 20 points to mean you don't feel lonely while 80 points would indicate strong feelings of loneliness. Most people score around 40 points. If your score is much higher than that, you should talk to a counselor or other trusted adult.[2]

Get out a notepad and see how your scores add up!

decide to call a friend, pick up a magazine or book, or go on the computer. You stop feeling lonely because you've become interested in something that has distracted you.

Your personality can also affect whether or not you feel lonely. A situation that might make one person feel lonely could cause no problems at all for someone else. For example, if you have an outgoing personality, moving from your old

Lonely Feelings Often Occur When...

1. You have lost a relationship.
2. You feel unneeded and different from others.
3. You don't think you have friends.
4. You feel misunderstood.
5. You've recently moved.
6. You have poor relationships with family or peers.
7. You are extremely shy or lack social skills to make friends.

Science Says...

All humans need to connect with others. From birth onward, social interactions are essential for normal development—and for survival itself. Viennese psychiatrist Rene Spitz came to this conclusion during the 1940s after comparing children in an orphanage with those living in a prison nursery. The children living in the orphanage received little attention, although their surroundings were clean and they were well fed. However, these children not only displayed

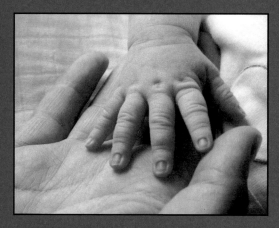

Your need to connect with other people begins at birth.

emotional and social disorders, but twenty-three of the eighty-eight institutionalized kids became sick and died. In contrast, all the children in the prison nursery—who were cuddled and able to form attachments with others—not only survived, but showed normal development.

neighborhood and changing schools might be easy for you. But if you are shy, you may have trouble trying to figure out unfamiliar social groups. Making new friends can be hard. One person may be devastated having lost the old familiar routine of life. Another person may react to change with excitement. Everyone is different.

Most people feel strong pangs of loneliness after the loss of something or someone important in their lives. You can feel pretty rotten after a conflict with a good friend, or a breakup with a girlfriend. If a relationship has permanently ended, it can hurt—a lot. Another very hard kind of loss to deal with is the death of someone you care about. It is normal to feel intense loneliness after this kind of loss.

When people lose someone they care about, they may steer clear of future relationships. In this way, they figure, they will not get hurt again. However, dealing with loneliness by withdrawing from people and not forming new friendships or relationships is not a good solution. Such actions are not healthy ways of coping with loss. Avoidance doesn't bring about solutions to problems. And it doesn't help you feel better.

Learning to cope. The teen years can be a tough time. At this time in your life, you are examining your values, trying new things, and reducing your emotional dependence on your parents. At the same time, you are establishing stronger and closer relationships with peers—the people of your own age. If those peers don't respond in a good way—if you feel rejected by them—it can be painful. After all, these are the people you are around the most and whose opinions you value.

At the same time, today's society makes it hard for boys to admit to having problems that cause emotional pain. Boys are expected to be "strong," and hide their emotions. This is especially true of emotions such as fear, hurt, or shame. These

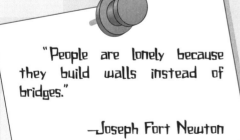

"People are lonely because they build walls instead of bridges."

—Joseph Fort Newton

Guys are typically expected to be tough and not show their emotions. As a result, they may withdraw or avoid sharing their feelings with others. Such actions can make feelings of loneliness worse.

so-called negative emotions are thought to show weakness. However, it is important that you learn to understand and express your emotions, no matter what they are. Your emotions affect your behavior with others. When you understand and accept your feelings, you can work through your problems. Ultimately, you'll feel better about yourself and have healthier relationships with others.

It can be hard to come out of your shell when you are feeling lonely. But the first step in overcoming loneliness is recognizing that certain actions, such as withdrawing and avoiding, only make things worse. There are healthier ways to deal with feelings of loneliness and to overcome them.

CHAPTER TWO

The Shy Guy

During the first week of school, Isaiah noticed the new girl in his English class. In fact, everyone seemed to notice Kara, with her curly dark hair and ready smile.

Since then, Kara has made a lot of friends in a short period of time. But Isaiah isn't one of them. Although he sits next to Kara in class, he hasn't really spoken to her. He thinks he'd like to get to know her. But whenever he looks her way, he freezes up and doesn't know what to say. He isn't sure how to break the ice.

saiah isn't alone. Most people find that shyness gets in the way of making friends. It makes it hard to break the ice—to find the words to start a conversation with someone you don't really know. One out of two Americans admits that shyness is what keeps them from connecting with others.[1]

What makes teens shy? The most common situations, teens say, are when they meet strangers, talk to authority figures, and try to talk to members of the opposite sex.[2] Shyness causes a range of emotions. The shy person feels uncomfortable, self-conscious, scared, or insecure. These feelings occur even before any conversation begins.

Isaiah gets nervous and shy around Kara.

Shyness

Shyness often worsens during times of change. For example, you may feel really shy on the first day of school. Or you are more likely to have shy feelings when meeting someone new. This can be especially true when you're attracted to the person. You also are more likely to feel shy in new situations in which you don't understand what is expected of you.

People who are mildly or moderately shy can usually work through their initial feelings of shyness in new situations. They force themselves to deal with their uncomfortable feelings. As they become involved in a conversation or speech, they generally find that their tense feelings disappear.

However, in the extremely shy person, such feelings don't melt away after a few minutes. It is too hard to push through the shyness. Extreme shyness can interfere with a person's ability to make friends or to date. Such feelings can prevent people from becoming who they want to be.

To break the ice means to remove the awkwardness or tension of a first meeting. The expression, which dates back more than 400 years, refers to the breaking up of river ice during the spring thaw. After warm temperatures melted the ice, boats on the river could pass through to their destinations.

What Causes Shyness?

Genes. Genes are units of heredity that help determine people's characteristics. Some scientists say the genes that children inherit from their parents can determine whether or not the kids are naturally shy. The shy personality can be apparent even when a person is very young. For example, shyness can keep a toddler from joining in a group activity right away. He or she may need to watch what's going on for awhile before feeling comfortable joining in.

Learned behaviors. The way a person has been taught to handle social situations can affect whether he or she feels shy. If the parents are uncomfortable in social situations, the child may also be uneasy. If the parents have difficulty talking to new people, the child may imitate the same behavior without even realizing it.

Previous experiences. If a person has been treated badly in the past, he or she will be shy around others. Someone who has been teased, bullied, or humiliated will tend to avoid situations in which such things could happen again.

When shyness is a problem. For many teens, extreme shyness can make them feel very isolated and alone. Because they don't think they can hold a conversation, they stop trying to talk. They become so overwhelmed with worry about what others might think of them that they don't speak up. They don't try new things, for fear of drawing attention to themselves.

The discomfort caused by shyness is easy to see in some people. They stammer and stutter as they try to find the right words. Their mistakes make them more nervous. They blush a

Some symptoms of shyness include nervousness, butterflies in the stomach, sweating, and stammering.

lot or sweat heavily. In a new social situation, they may feel so embarrassed that all they can think about is how to escape the conversation or situation. Because talking to strangers is so painful, many extremely shy people simply retreat into their shells. They avoid social situations.

Some shy teens may appear calm and self-confident on the outside. But they are actually terribly nervous and unhappy on the inside. That's because they can't stop thinking about how they look. Or they are worrying about how the conversation is going. Or they are wondering whether the person they are talking to likes them. The fear of being embarrassed in social situations can make shy people come across as abrupt and unfriendly. (Although fortunately, it is possible to learn how to respond differently in such situations.)

Certain situations cause a physical response in the person who feels extreme shyness. This response is the fear reaction. In a social situation, the body and mind are reacting to an apparent danger. The danger is not real. But the fear reaction

Social Phobia

One out of ten people can experience extreme shyness, anxiety, and stress called social phobia. Feelings of fear are so strong that they interfere with the person's ability to relate to others. When untreated, the person with social phobia withdraws and avoids other people. So the disorder tends to grow worse. Treatment typically involves therapy. The person learns new social skills and ways to manage anxiety and reduce stress.

Loneliness

It can be hard to get a conversation going when you are with a group of people you don't really know. Try to relax and be yourself. You never know where you might meet your new best friend.

can cause a racing heart rate, weak knees, dizziness, and clammy hands. Symptoms of shyness can also include having a queasy feeling in the abdomen. This pain is often referred to as having "butterflies in the stomach."

Low self-esteem. Many shy people suffer from low self-esteem. The term *self-esteem* refers to the way you feel and think about yourself. If you have low self-esteem, you don't believe you have much to offer others. You may think that people don't want you around.

A guy with low self-esteem may think there is something wrong with him. He thinks that explains why people don't like him. Because he doesn't like himself, he figures no one is going

Using "People Skills"

Be prepared. Practice what you are going to say before beginning a conversation. That way, the words will come more easily to you when you want to start talking.

Be aware of your body language. Be approachable. Remember that body language can make a shy person seem angry or rude. Try to act friendly, even when you are feeling very nervous—or left out. Face the speaker and look into his or her eyes. Be relaxed, but pay close attention.

When talking to a person, maintain eye contact. Show you are interested in what the person has to say. As the person speaks, try to feel what he or she is feeling. Keep an open mind.

Make it clear you are listening. Don't interrupt. Nod your head as the person speaks and say, "uh huh." If you don't understand something, wait until the speaker pauses and then ask him or her to explain. ("What do you mean by…?")

Handshakes feed the basic human need for physical contact.

to like him, either. Even when people act friendly toward him, he may suspect their motives. The shy guy may think that the only reason they're paying any attention to him is because they want something. He may think that they don't really like him for who he is.

Overcoming shyness. You may believe that you fall into the category of the extremely shy person. However, you can still make friends. The first step is to recognize your shy feelings and then push through them. One way to do that is to work on improving your "people skills." These are the techniques you can use when interacting with others.

Work at making small talk. If you don't feel competent making conversation, listen in on the small talk others are having. Then, once you think you have the right idea, force yourself to practice these same skills.

When you have a conversation, try not to be self-conscious. But make sure your body language shows you are interested in what the other person is saying: Look him or her in the eye. When you look at the floor, you are sending a signal that says you don't care what the other person is saying. Stand up straight and tall, and smile. Even if you don't feel confident, do your best to look like you are feeling self-assured and in

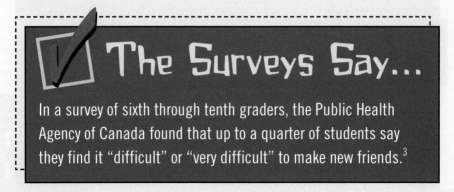

The Surveys Say...

In a survey of sixth through tenth graders, the Public Health Agency of Canada found that up to a quarter of students say they find it "difficult" or "very difficult" to make new friends.[3]

Some Strategies Used by Teens to Overcome Shyness

"Tried making conversation with people I would like to know."
   (72 percent)

"Tried going to public places (e.g., mall, dances, park) to meet people."
   (44 percent)

"Joined activities outside school." (39 percent)

"Joined clubs or extracurricular activities in school." (37 percent)

"Used alcohol or drugs." (24 percent)

"Had individual therapy or counseling." (8 percent)

"Read self-help books." (4 percent)[4]

control. Try to act like you are comfortable with the situation (even if you're not). You may find that with time—and practice—you actually will become a little more relaxed in new social situations.

You can find opportunities to practice by joining an after-school club or activity that involves groups of people. But don't join just any club. Pick one that involves something you like to do. For example, if you like playing chess, join the chess club at school. Conversations should go easier when you share common interests.

Be prepared. When you know a possibly uncomfortable social situation is coming up, practice ahead of time. Plan what you'll say or do. For example, if you are thinking of asking the girl in your science class if she'd like to go to the school dance with you, rehearse what you'll say next time you see her. You could write down what you want to say. Or you could practice the conversation in front of the mirror. Be sure to take the next step, though, and actually follow through on that conversation.

Think positive. Try to stop being so hard on yourself. Don't think negative thoughts about how you look or imagine the bad things that others may be thinking about you. Find something positive about yourself. What are you good at? What are your qualities and strengths? Be your own best friend. You would want to give a good friend some support before he or she tried a difficult task, right? Treat yourself the same way. When you are about to deal with a potentially uncomfortable situation, give yourself a compliment and encouragement.

Be assertive. Being assertive means standing up for and expressing what you believe in. But it also means being respectful of others' opinions and beliefs. Being assertive can be hard for the shy person who is caught up with worry about what other people are thinking. But if you believe strongly in something, you need to speak up in an assertive way. You will feel better about yourself.

Avoid avoidance. Sure, it may be easier to avoid situations that make you uncomfortable. But doing that won't help you learn how to cope with shy feelings. By putting yourself forward into situations that make you feel shy—and forcing yourself to stay in them—you will get used to them. Replace old patterns of avoiding conversations with new experiences of participating in them. With practice, you may find it easier to think of things to say. These behaviors you learn and practice today will help you for the rest of your life.

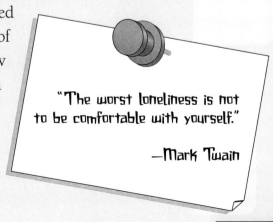

"The worst loneliness is not to be comfortable with yourself."

—Mark Twain

CHAPTER THREE

Building Friendships

A friend is someone you can relax with and be yourself. Friends can be a source of fun—people to share good times with. And friends can provide understanding, support, and guidance when you're having trouble. During the teen years, you can often be more comfortable talking with friends rather than with family about issues and problems. You may find you relate better with friends because friends often are going through the same kinds of situations and having similar feelings.

However, if you have difficulty making and keeping friends, some of the suggestions in this chapter can help. Keep them in mind the next time you are talking to classmates and other peers. Remember, what is most important in forming relationships with other people is that you be yourself. Don't pretend to be someone you're not.

Initiate the conversation. If you see someone you'd like to get to know better, make the first move. Say hello and smile. Make a comment about the upcoming class test, yesterday's basketball game, or even the weather. Don't wait for the other person to talk first.

"A real friend is one who walks in when the rest of the world walks out."

—Walter Winchell

Show you are interested in what the other person is saying. Once a conversation has begun, continue it by asking questions and listening to the answers. Ask the other person about what he

If you see someone sitting alone, go sit down and introduce yourself. The person will appreciate your effort, although at first he or she may be just as nervous about talking as you.

or she thinks. People appreciate it when you show an interest in them and what they have to say. Learn to be a good listener.

Give and take. Share your own thoughts and opinions. But be respectful when others have ideas and opinions that differ from yours. You don't want to make friends only with people who think exactly like you do, although it is likely you'll be attracted to people who share your values.

Choose your friends wisely. Every school has its groups or cliques. They typically form when teens with similar interests, values, and personalities hang out together. They may join a group because they feel comfortable with its members. But sometimes teens look to join groups for the wrong reasons—to be with the guys who are thought to be popular or who are top athletes.

Take your time in choosing your friends. Avoid joining a group simply because it has an identity you think you'd like to have. And don't keep company with people you don't really like or respect—just because you think no one else is around.

Over time, acquaintances can become good friends—and good friends can become better friends.

Characteristics of a Good Friend

- Can be trusted not to betray a confidence
- Shows an interest in you and is concerned about your problems
- Is supportive and helps out when needed
- Celebrates your successes
- Is honest
- Has a good sense of humor

Instead, try to develop friendships with people who are supportive and understanding. Avoid people who constantly tease you or make you feel bad about yourself. Don't make friends with people who like to gossip about others or put them down. You may find that you become the object of their harassment. Similarly, steer clear of those who try to make you do things that you don't want to do or that you think are wrong.

Building good friendships takes time. Remember, being good friends with a person involves sharing a part of yourself. It involves both giving and receiving trust. That means you don't talk about your friend with others. And you don't expect that friend to talk about you, either. If a friend has told you something in confidence, you don't tell other people unless you are concerned for the friend's safety. In that case, you should tell a parent or other trusted adult.

CHAPTER FOUR

Feeling Rejected and Depressed

> *Seth has been unhappy since the first day of middle school, when for some reason he got on the bad side of Kevin and his friends. At school, they picked on Seth for being so bad at sports. But the teasing was worse when he was at home on the computer. At Kevin's prompting, other kids from school bombarded Seth's computer with insulting messages. Someone posted an embarrassing picture of him on a Web site.*

Being rejected by peers hurts. And the sadness and isolation that a victim of bullying feels can hurt a lot. The effects of feeling isolated and rejected can last a long time—well into adulthood.

Being bullied. Bullying can be physical assaults such as hitting, punching, or shoving. Or it can involve having one's belongings taken or damaged. It can also be verbal assaults such as name-calling, teasing, or threats of physical abuse. A more recent form of bullying is cyberbullying. It involves teasing, insults, and threats that are text-messaged on cell phones or that appear on Web sites.

Approximately 15 to 25 percent of U.S. students say they are bullied frequently. Another 15 to 20 percent say that they bully others.[1]

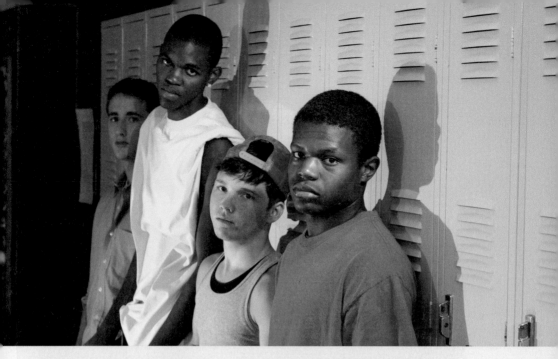

Don't be a victim of bullies. You can get support from family, friends, and school staff. But you have to let people know what is going on.

Bullies often pick on kids who are seen as different. The victim of bullying may be overweight or have a disability. A guy may be picked on because he's not athletic, or because he's seen as being "too smart." Regardless of the "reason" for being bullied, the victim feels deep pain and loneliness because of rejection. Often the guy who is the victim of bullying blames himself. He thinks that there must be something wrong with him. It is hard for him to realize the truth—that the problem is with the bully, not with him.

When bullying goes on for a long time, it makes its victim feel isolated and alone. Kids who are subjected to months and years of bullying figure they have no alternative but to avoid situations where it takes place. So they often skip school or simply drop out.

Depression and loneliness. Being tormented and teased by bullies can wear anyone down. If you're constantly hearing negative comments about yourself, you can easily begin

Feeling Rejected and Depressed

If You Are Being Bullied

1. Don't keep your feelings to yourself. Talk to a trusted friend or adult.

2. Be aware that the bullying is not likely to go away on its own.

3. Confront the bully and ask her or him to stop, if you feel safe doing that.

4. If the bullying continues, talk to an adult about what is going on.

to believe what is being said and lose confidence in yourself. Ongoing feelings of loneliness and low self-esteem can lead to even more serious problems such as major depression.

Clinical depression is a form of major depression. It is diagnosed when feelings of extreme sadness last for more than two weeks. A guy with clinical depression is typically in a sad mood all the time. He is irritable and has feelings of hopelessness. Other symptoms of clinical depression may include emotional instability, extreme mood swings, and the lack of ability to focus on daily tasks. Some psychologists believe that symptoms of depression for men can also include angry outbursts, withdrawal, and risk-taking behaviors.

"It is loneliness that makes the loudest noise. This is true of men as of dogs."

—Eric Hoffer

Because men and boys are socialized to not show emotions, they try to ignore them. If they are suffering from severe depression, trying to ignore emotions can be a serious problem. Psychologist William Pollack notes,

"Men not only don't get treatment, they try to convince themselves they don't have an illness."[2] Because they don't acknowledge their pain, guys tend to express negative feelings with violence. They may direct it toward themselves with self-destructive behavior and recklessness. Or they may act violently toward others. In some cases, they turn to drugs to "self-medicate" their emotional pain.

In teenagers, depression often occurs with other disorders such as anxiety, eating disorders, and substance abuse. Depression has also been found to lead to increased risk for suicide.[3] Men commit suicide at four times the rate than that of women,[4] a statistic that to some experts means symptoms of depression in men and boys aren't being recognized.

"Cynically Shy"

Researcher Bernardo Carducci reports that the connection between shyness and bullying doesn't apply only to shy teens being targets. He found that certain teens are what the researchers call "cynically shy." That is, their shyness not only makes them uncomfortable, but angry. As a result, they turn into bullies themselves. "They feel frustrated and hostile because they can't connect," Carducci says. "When you feel that isolated, you can begin to have hostile feelings toward others. . . . And it's very easy to go from hating people to hurting people." The researcher believes that some cynically shy teens have gone on to horrific acts, including shootings in schools.[5]

Clinical Depression

Bullying is not the only stressful situation that can lead to depression. People typically feel sad when other difficult crises occur, such as a parent's divorce, breakup with a good friend, or the death of a loved one. In most cases, the result will be a bad mood and a short period of feeling down. However, when depression lasts for more than two weeks, it is considered clinical depression.

Major depression is treatable. Studies have shown that the most effective treatment is a combination of medications and psychotherapy, or "talk therapy."[6] Through one form of talk therapy, a medical professional works with the patient to try to change negative styles of thinking and behaving. Another kind of therapy involves helping the patient improve troubled personal relationships.

Signs of Depression

These symptoms usually occur every day over a period of at least two weeks:

Emotional: prolonged sadness, emptiness, low self-esteem, guilt, or thoughts of suicide and death.

Physical: sleep and appetite disorders, headaches, or stomachaches.

Behavioral: isolating self from others; acting out anger; conflicts with friends, parents, or at school; turning to alcohol or drug abuse.[7]

Science Says...

Depression is a biochemical disorder that affects the body's neurotransmitters. Neurotransmitters are special chemicals that carry messages between brain cells in the brain. Depression occurs when neurotransmitters such as serotonin and dopamine, which affect the emotions, are out of balance. The disorder requires quick medical attention.

If you think you may have problems with depression or you have a friend whom you believe is suffering from depression, you should talk to an adult. He or she can help you or your friend obtain help from a trained mental health professional. This person can figure out what is causing the depression and prescribe appropriate therapy or medication.

Take action against feelings of loneliness. Many guys detach themselves from a situation when they face problems. They find it difficult to discuss their feelings with others, considering it a sign of weakness. But they need

"Always keep an open mind and a compassionate heart."

—Phil Jackson

to recognize that admitting to their feelings is actually a courageous thing to do.

Even though it may be difficult, try to talk to others about what you are experiencing. Push yourself to talk to somebody else about the way you feel. Don't shut yourself off from family and friends, but instead try to reach out and improve your relationship with at least one other person, especially a person whom you trust. Ask for feedback from others about whether your behavior could be contributing to your problems with others. Ask for advice on what to do.

Be open and willing to accept that person's thoughts. And follow through. If you don't try to take some kind of positive action, it is possible things can become worse.

Science Says...

Loneliness can be bad for your health. Psychology professor John Cacioppo and researchers from the University of Chicago and Ohio State University have reported that lonely people have a harder time handling stress than people who aren't lonely. They tend to feel threatened, rather than challenged, by stressful situations. The feeling of being threatened leads to high blood pressure, which in turn affects heart function and disrupts sleep.[8]

Unhealthy Ways of Coping

There are several unhealthy ways of dealing with loneliness. Some guys deny there is a problem at all. They don't try to form relationships or make friends. Instead, they may obsess over celebrities and sports stars, or spend all their free time in front of the television set or computer. Some people may try to escape from unhappy or lonely feelings by using drugs or alcohol.

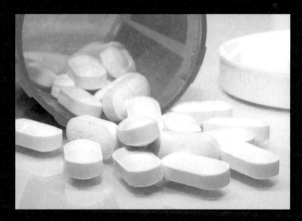

If you think your friend is using drugs, talk about it. Encourage him to get help.

Instead of allowing loneliness to lead to anger or hostility, you can ease your feelings when you talk about them. When you connect with your problem, you have a better likelihood of finding a solution.

CHAPTER FIVE

When Loss Causes Loneliness

Jason is having a hard time. Last year, his father moved out of the house, and a few months ago, his parents' divorce was finalized. Although Jason sees his father on weekends, he misses spending time with him. Meanwhile, his mother has much less time to spend with either Jason or his little brother. She is often too busy with her new job and with chores to talk to Jason. He misses the times when the whole family used to sit down together at the dinner table, and often wishes his life would return to the way it used to be.

When you lose someone who is important to you, it can leave a hole in your life. Jason feels sad and lonely because the divorce means he no longer sees his father every day. Feelings of loneliness can occur because of other kinds of life changes, too, such as the death of a close family member or friend or a breakup with someone important to you. Such events can cause a range of emotions, including sadness and fear—as well as emotional loneliness.

Loss because of divorce. It is estimated that each year the parents of one million American kids get divorced.[1] In total, some 20 million kids under the age of eighteen live in homes in which their parents have decided to separate or divorce.[2] In other words, there are a lot of kids like Jason.

If you are dealing with your parents' separation or divorce, you may also be experiencing loneliness and depression. You may feel that your parents are too wrapped up in

Losing someone close to you can trigger a range of emotions. It's perfectly normal to feel sad and to grieve.

their problems. Or that they aren't there to connect with you and your needs. Even if the divorce has been over and done with for many years, you still may feel isolated from your parents.

The Surveys Say...

According to statistics for 2002, 10 percent of the American population is divorced, up from 8 percent in 1990 and 6 percent in 1980.[3]

Sometimes kids whose parents are divorcing blame themselves for the breakup. Because they believe the divorce is their fault, they avoid talking about it and how it makes them feel. As a result, they can feel terribly lonely and isolated. It is important to remember that when separations and divorces occur, they happen because of the couple's problems with each other. Breakups are not the fault of the kids.

Dealing with changes. Many changes in family life can occur because of divorce. Depending on the custody agreement, visits with one parent may be limited. As a result, you won't see as much of one of your parents as you did before the divorce. You may be shuttling back and forth between both your mother's place and your father's home. Or you may be living with only one parent. One or both of your parents may have remarried. That means you may be having to learn to deal with a whole new set of family members—stepsiblings or half- brothers and half-sisters.

In addition, the separation and divorce may have caused financial problems for the parent you live with. Without the income of both parents, there may not be enough money to support the household. This may mean you and your family have to move to where housing is less expensive.

A new family situation and moving to a new neighborhood are major changes. When you must deal with a lot of changes, you can feel a great deal of stress. And if at the same time you don't think anyone cares about what you are going through, it can be really hard. That's where feelings of loneliness can kick in—when you feel like you have no one to talk to. No one understands what you are going through.

Psychologists believe that divorce can be very difficult on boys, who often live with the mothers as the result of custody decisions. The divorce can mean a son spends little time with his father. Instead of expressing feelings of disappointment over no longer living with their dad, many boys feel as though they have to "tough it out." They don't talk about how they feel isolated and lonely. Additional pressure to "side with" their mother or become the man of the house can also contribute to feelings of aloneness, alienation from dad, and being different from other guys.

When you experience a loss, the feelings can be quite strong. It's okay to let them out.

Grief and loss. Feelings of isolation and loneliness can be particularly strong after the death of a family member or close friend. When someone close to you dies, you lose having the person around and involved in your life. Your reaction can vary. The initial shock can overwhelm you with terrible grief, or the sense of missing the person may come in waves that occur at unexpected times. Or you may be surprised to find you react with very little emotion. Such feelings are all normal, although painful.

Grief is a normal and healthy reaction to loss. It is normal to cry and feel sad and depressed when someone close to you dies. Grieving the death of a loved one doesn't mean you are suffering from major depression. However, coping with your sorrow can take time—weeks, months, and even years.

When someone close to you passes away, you can feel overwhelmed. Everyone grieves differently, but it's important to acknowledge your feelings by talking with others.

Psychologist Elisabeth Kübler-Ross observed the feelings of people with terminal illnesses or experiencing the death of loved ones. She described these feelings of grief as occurring in five stages:

Denial: "This can't be happening."

Anger: "Why is this happening? Whose fault is it?"

Bargaining: "I promise to _____, if my friend lives."

Depression: "I'm too sad to do anything."

Acceptance: "What has happened or will happen can't be changed. I'm at peace with it and ready to move on."

It is necessary to go through the stages of grief—as painful as they can be—according to your own schedule in order to come to terms with your loss.

Loss with the breakup of a relationship. The same feelings of grief and loneliness that occur with the death of someone close to you can also occur with the breakup of a relationship. It is normal to feel lonely when a relationship—whether a close friendship or a romantic relationship—comes to an end.

When someone you love and care about has chosen to break up with you, your sense of loss can be overwhelming.

When you can begin to understand and label the emotions you are feeling, you can better control and use them in a positive way.

Helping Others Cope with Loss

If you have a friend who has recently broken up with someone, you can provide support to make the person feel better. Offer your support and companionship. But let your friend do most of the talking. Be aware that he or she will be moody—filled with grief, anger, confusion, and negative feelings. Let your friend know that you understand and will be there if needed.

Although it can be uncomfortable being around someone going through pain and difficulty, your presence can mean a lot. It shows your friend that he or she is not alone.

Feelings of numbness and disbelief that the breakup has occurred are followed by pain. You may feel physically sick, lose your appetite, and have difficulty concentrating on other things. Eventually, feelings of anger against the person give way to loneliness and despair. It's natural to start longing for the way things used to be.

It can be hard to think well of yourself if the other person is the one deciding it was time to break up. This can be especially true when you weren't even aware of a problem. As a result, some guys turn on themselves when a relationship ends. They believe that if they had only been smarter, better looking, or richer, then things would have worked out.

Keep in mind that breakups seldom occur because of one reason or character trait. More typically they occur because at least one of you has changed. Rather than spend energy obsessing over how to renew a lost relationship, acknowledge it is over and move on. Be patient with yourself. With time, you'll be able to think better about tomorrow. Getting over a breakup

Loneliness

can take a matter of days or it can take months—the amount of time you need depends on how you deal with your emotions and on how strong or important the relationship was to you.

Coping with loss. Your emotional reactions to loss are normal, but you may be feeling overwhelmed by them. To stay healthy during such stressful times, it is important that you take care of yourself.

To minimize the effects of stress on your body, take care of yourself physically. Get lots of sleep, eat healthy foods, and exercise regularly. You'll still be sad, but staying healthy can help you avoid becoming severely depressed. Keep yourself busy—work on a hobby, get together with friends to watch a movie or play a basketball game, listen to music, or go for a run.

You will need to think about what happened, but try not to dwell on your loss. Deal directly with your feelings, and try to "process" them. Pay attention to your emotions. Name what you

When to Get Help

It's time to get help if a friend experiences any of the following:

- Spends an excessive amount of time alone
- Shows a lack of interest in daily activities
- Experiences changes in sleeping and eating habits
- Uses drugs or alcohol to numb feelings
- Threatens to harm himself or herself
- Engages in risky behavior

Coping with any type of loss can be difficult. However, you can try to keep your mind off your grief by staying busy.

are feeling and accept that it exists. Then, after holding and accepting the feeling for a few minutes, consciously try to let it go.

For example, you may identify that you are feeling angry. Consciously acknowledging the anger will help you see how it is affecting your behavior. Perhaps you are pushing people away because you are lashing out at them. So they are steering clear of you. As a result of your behavior, your feelings of isolation and loneliness are intensifying. Once you process that you are feeling angry, you can try to change your behavior—and reconnect with others who may be able to help you.

What you don't want to do is to try to deaden the pain of loss by using alcohol or drugs. To get over the pain of loss, you need to deal with it. When you use alcohol and drugs instead of working through your emotions, you are numbing yourself to your feelings. They will continue to build up inside and stay with you. Using alcohol and drugs don't provide long-lasting

The Surveys Say...

Americans today have fewer friendships than they used to, says a survey published in the *American Sociological Review*. The authors of the study found that the average person in 2004 had two close friends, compared with three close friends in 1985. One in four people interviewed by the authors of the 2004 study said they had no close friends at all.[4]

solutions. They only invite more problems since their use by teens is also illegal.

To help lessen the pain of loneliness caused by loss, talk to other people. By sharing your feelings with someone who understands what you're going through, you'll feel better. This person can be a good friend or family member you can easily talk to. Your problems need to be heard, and when you share your concerns with others, you may also hear advice that you hadn't thought of.

As with the pain caused by breakups, the grief caused by loss will be helped with the passage of time. You can also benefit by accepting and working through the emotions you are feeling.

Sharing feelings can be tough for guys. You may feel more comfortable talking to a female friend or relative, such as an older sister. Or you may find it helpful to talk to a school counselor, psychologist, or a clergy person. Sometimes, just hanging out with friends can help take your mind off the hurt and any negative feelings you are having.

CHAPTER SIX

Choosing to Be Alone

When Jake is done with school each day, he comes home to an empty house. His mother, who now works the evening shift, had asked him if he would have preferred going to a friend's house after school each day instead. But at age thirteen, Jake feels okay with the way things are. Every day, as soon as he walks through the door, he makes sure to call his mother to let her know he's home. Then he typically grabs a bite to eat, takes the dog for a walk, and takes care of chores. He figures that if he doesn't take care of his responsibilities, his parents might not want him home after school by himself anymore. And he likes having time alone.

Just because you are alone doesn't mean you are lonely. Many kids with working parents spend time by themselves when they come home for school. This time by themselves can be a real plus. It can give them a chance to think without interruption, read, study, or work on homework or hobbies.

There are other ways you might choose solitude—time when you are alone. Sometimes you might prefer to stay at home rather than attend the school dance or attend a movie with the rest of your friends. You might prefer to spend the

Solitude is the state of being alone and secluded from other people. It typically occurs because of a conscious choice to be alone.

You can be productive while you're alone. Catch up on some homework, or on the latest sports scores.

time doing something on your own—reading a book, playing music, or writing a computer program.

Just because you want to be by yourself doesn't make you lonely. Feelings of loneliness occur when you are sad about the situation. Someone who chooses to be alone doesn't feel unhappy and wish things were different.

Extroverts and introverts. Personality plays a part in how you feel about being by yourself. There are two main kinds of personalities: the extrovert and the introvert.

"I never found the companion that was so companionable as solitude."

—Henry David Thoreau

Are You an Extrovert or Introvert?

An Extrovert:

    . . . is talkative and open.

    . . . likes to think out loud.

    . . . shows emotions.

    . . . acts before thinking.

    . . . likes to be with people.

    . . . has lots of energy.

    . . . is outgoing.

An Introvert:

    . . . is quiet and thoughtful.

    . . . listens more than talks.

    . . . keeps emotions private.

    . . . thinks before acting.

    . . . prefers to work "behind-the-scenes."

    . . . likes to spend time alone.

    . . . is reserved.

Extroverts are outgoing individuals who thrive in crowded situations and enjoy working in busy, stimulating environments. They gain energy by being among people. However, they tend to feel very lonely and drained when they have to spend a lot of time alone.

In contrast, introverts like spending time alone, although they are not necessarily shy or lonely. They get energy from being on their own rather than being with large groups of people. When in crowds, they often feel drained of energy. Introverts like to work alone, rather than in groups. Solitude allows them to pursue activities such as writing, drawing, or painting.

Time for independent thinking. Working alone can help you become an independent thinker. There is nothing wrong with working with others—that builds an appreciation for teamwork. However, a lot can be said for learning how to do things on your own. By working alone, you have a chance to develop and nurture your own ideas.

Solitude can be a time when you review your thoughts and goals and decide what is important for you. When you work

When You're Home Alone

If you are home alone after school and find yourself a little bored and lonely, you can always find something to do. Things to do can include:

- Homework
- Chores
- Reading a book or magazine
- Working on a hobby
  - Listening to or playing music
  - Writing a letter
  - Phoning a friend
  - Using the computer

Use your alone time for reading and getting homework and assignments done.

Too Much Time Alone on the Computer?

Some people are concerned that teens are spending too much time on online activities such as multi-user games, instant messaging, and chat rooms. Some studies show that introverted kids who excessively play online games based on role-playing (acting out the role of another character) become isolated from friends and peers.

According to a study by the Stanford Institute for the Quantitative Study of Society, the more time people spend online, the less time they give to real-life relationships with family and friends. One of the study's authors blamed the Internet for having "an increasingly isolating effect on society."[1]

Others disagree. They point out that while 36 percent of Americans log on to the computer for more than five hours per week, approximately 60 percent of them say they spend less time watching TV.[2] In addition, using e-mail was the most popular activity. In other words, the Internet defenders say, people are *more connected* with friends and family because of e-mail.

on a project on your own, you can also gain confidence in yourself and your abilities to finish something on your own. Being on your own can also give you the opportunity to show that you can take care of yourself.

Time for creativity. In a 2005 survey, Americans were asked to finish the sentence, "My most creative ideas come when . . ." More than half of the respondents chose "in solitude" as the answer.[3] Most experts agree that solitude provides the quiet time that gives people the opportunity to come up with creative solutions to problems. That "alone time" provides a time for insights and for following wherever your own natural curiosity and imagination take you. Studies find that creative, imaginative people such as artists, musicians, and writers are at their most productive when they work alone.

Use your time alone to explore your creative abilities.

Taking time out. Many psychologists believe that people benefit when they have the chance to take "time out" and be on their own. This time spent away from other people can give them the opportunity to take an "emotional breather." They can think about themselves and their relationships with others. Or they can practice a favorite hobby. In general, having time to yourself can give you the opportunity to think without distractions from others.

"Man's loneliness is but his fear of life."

—Eugene O'Neill

Overcoming Loneliness

Loneliness can affect you in many different ways. You can feel a little lonely when you're simply bored and not sure what you want to do with yourself. And you can feel extremely lonely if you feel rejected and unwanted. A lack of friends may make you think something is wrong with you, which in turn can make you self-conscious, ill at ease, or even angry with others. A breakup or the death of a close friend or family member can result in feelings of loneliness, as well as anger, sadness, and grief.

So what do you do? If your loneliness is the result of wanting a close friendship or relationship, many of the same tips for overcoming shyness apply: These tips for overcoming loneliness boil down to developing the social skills that help you form close relationships.

Tips for Overcoming Loneliness

- Be aware of how you relate to others.
- Practice your people skills.
- Be the one to start a conversation.
- Get involved in classroom discussions and conversations.
- Don't avoid social situations. In fact, go out of your way to meet new people.

Remember, the more people you talk to, the better the odds of finding a good friend. Schools have many clubs, sports teams, and other extracurricular activities. Look for an activity that interests you and join. Not only will you meet new people, but you'll find friends who share the same interests.

You can also meet new people and practice inter-personal skills by working in a service job. In the restaurant business, for example, you have contact with many different people in a somewhat structured environment. You may also have the opportunity to learn skills on how to deal with people who are different from you.

The way you respond to your loneliness can affect your life and your relationships with others.

One of the best ways to overcome your own loneliness, experts say, is by helping others. By spending time with other people, especially those living in assisted care or hospitals, you can help reduce their feelings of loneliness. Be a volunteer in a service organization and do something to help out in your community. As you

Ways That Teens Cope with Loneliness

Teens say that they use various ways to cope with loneliness—some are helpful and some are harmful. The unhealthy ways do nothing to help to solve the problem.

Harmful

- **Feel sad and withdraw:** Cry, sleep, watch TV, do nothing.
- **Try to numb bad feelings:** Turn to drugs or alcohol.
- **Spend money:** Buy things to make themselves feel better.

Helpful

- **Seek solitude:** Work, read, write, listen to music, exercise, get involved with a hobby.
- **Give self pep talks:** Say things like, "These feelings won't last forever," and "I have good qualities that someone will see."
- **Reach out to others:** Call or visit a friend, help someone, or join a new activity.

increase your contact with other people, you won't feel as isolated. And at the same time, you will feel good about yourself for helping to make the world a better place.

Keep your existing friendships healthy. Be aware of your behavior—are you acting like the kind of friend you would want to have? If not, clean up your act. Do your best to be there for your friends when they need you.

Join a community or school sports team. You'll have the chance to make some friends, gain some confidence, and improve your skills.

Go out of your way to talk to friends and family members. Although you may enjoy hobbies such as watching television, reading books, and surfing the Internet, be sure to take time to live in the real world. Participate in your school and community activities and visit people you care about.

Remember that everyone has feelings of loneliness at one time or another. Even those people who seem very confident

Is Your Behavior Ruining Friendships?

1. Do you get angry with others easily?

2. When you are with a group of friends and they decide to play ball when you would rather do something else, do you go home instead of joining in the game?

3. Instead of letting minor problems pass, do you hold a grudge?

4. When you are angry with your friends, do you give them the silent treatment?

5. Be honest. Would you like to be friends with the person who answers "yes" to all of these questions?

and self-assured will admit to feeling lonely and scared about certain things. If you're nervous about starting a conversation with the student standing next to you in the lunch line, keep in mind that the other person is probably feeling as self-conscious or uncertain as you are.

Conversation Starters

Ask open-ended questions (questions that require more than yes or no for an answer). Instead of saying, "Do you like that television show? (easily answered by yes or no), say "Why do you think that show is such a big hit?"

You can make new friends by joining an afterschool tutoring program or helping with your school newspaper.

If you've spent your life avoiding situations that make you uncomfortable, forcing yourself to behave differently can feel like taking a step off a cliff. But if you believe you aren't any good at making friends, then you probably won't be! Practice replacing those negative thoughts with more positive ones. And keep trying to connect and get to know new people. With persistence, you are bound to find the people with whom you feel really comfortable. So, stay active and keep reaching out to others.

" No one would choose a friend-less existence on condition of having all the other things in the world."

—Aristotle

CHAPTER NOTES

Chapter 1. Understanding Loneliness

1. Mark Dolliver, "It's Not All Root Beer and Skittles, But a High Schooler's Life Isn't Bad," *Adweek*, August 22, 2005, p. 25.

2. Dan Russell, Letitia A. Peplau, and Carolyn E. Cutrona, "The Revised UCLA Loneliness Scale: Concurrent and Discriminant Validity Evidence," *Journal of Personality and Social Psychology*, September 1980.

Chapter 2. The Shy Guy

1. Bernardo Carducci and Philip G. Zimbardo, "Are You Shy?" *Psychology Today*, November/December 1995, <http://psychologytoday.com/articles/pto-19951101-000030.html> (March 24, 2008).

2. Lauren J. Bryant, "Fighting Shy," *Indiana University: Research & Creative Activity*, Spring 2003, <http://www.indiana.edu/~rcapub/v25n2/carducci.shtml> (March 11, 2008).

3. Public Health Agency of Canada, "Chapter 4: Peer Relationships," September 2, 2002, <http://www.phac-aspc.gc.ca/dca-dea/publications/hbsc_04_e.html> (March 24, 2008).

4. Percentages do not add up to 100 percent because the survey allowed for the selection of more than one strategy. From Bernardo J. Carducci et al., "How Shy Teens Deal with Shyness: Strategic and Gender Differences," *Poster Session*, American Psychological Association, Toronto, Canada, August 2003.

Chapter 4. Feeling Rejected and Depressed

1. U.S. Department of Health and Human Services, "Effects of Bullying," *Stop Bullying Now!* n.d., <http://www.stopbullying-now.hrsa.gov/index.asp?area=effects> (March 11, 2008).

2. Nancy Wartik, "Depression Comes Out of Hiding," *New York Times*, June 25, 2000, Special section 16, p.1.

3. "Depression," *National Institute of Mental Health*, March 13, 2008, <http://www.nimh.nih.gov/health/publications/depression/complete-publication.shtml> (March 18, 2008).

4. Wartik, "Depression Comes Out of Hiding."

5. Lauren J. Bryant, "Fighting Shy," *Research & Creative Activity*, Spring 2003, <http://www.indiana.edu/~rcapub/v25n2/carducci.shtml> (March 11, 2008).

6. "Depression," *National Institute of Mental Health*, March 13, 2008, <http://www.nimh.nih.gov/health/publications/depression/complete-publication.shtml> (March 18, 2008).

7. "Young & the Lonely: A Team of Top Experts Answers Your Questions About Loneliness and Depression," *Science World*, February 7, 2003, p. 18.

8. Bill Harms, "New Research Reveals How Loneliness Can Undermine Health," *The University of Chicago Chronicle*, August 17, 2000, <http://chronicle.uchicago.edu/000817/loneliness.shtml> (April 16, 2008).

Chapter 5. When Loss Causes Loneliness

1. Walter Kim, "Should You Stay Together for the Kids?" *Time*, September 25, 2000, p. 74.

2. Rose M. Kreider, "Living Arrangements of Children: 2004," *Current Population Reports*, February 2008, <http://www.census.gov/prod/2008pubs/p70-114.pdf> (March 12, 2008).

3. "U.S. Divorce Statistics," *Divorce Magazine*, n.d., <http://www.divorcemag.com/statistics/statsUS.shtml> (March 13, 2008).

4. Janet Kornblum, "Study: 25 Percent of Americans Have No One to Confide In," *USA Today*, June 26, 2006, <http://www.usatoday.com/news/nation/2006-06-22-friendship_x.htm> (March 12, 2008).

Chapter 6. Choosing to Be Alone

1. Joellen Perry, "Only the Cyberlonely," *U.S. News & World Report*, February 28, 2000, p. 62.

2. Ibid.

3. Judy Hevrdejs, "Accelerate Thinking Creatively in the Car," *Chicago Tribune*, February 20, 2005, p. 2.

anxiety—Feelings of fear, apprehension, and worry.

biochemical—Describing the branch of science concerned with chemical processes that take place in living organisms.

body language—A nonverbal form of communication involving facial expressions, gestures, and movements that often reveal what a person is really thinking or feeling.

depression—Extreme sadness; clinical depression is a mental disorder in which feelings of sadness, hopelessness, and loss of interest in life last for more than two weeks.

emotional loneliness—Loneliness resulting from not feeling close with another person or able to depend on someone else.

extrovert—A person with an outgoing personality.

genes—The basic units of heredity that help determine a person's characteristics, or traits.

introvert—A person who is quiet and has self-reliant qualities.

loneliness—Feelings of sadness because of a lack of company or a strong emotional connection to someone else.

negative emotion—An unpleasant emotion or feeling (such as anger, fear, or shame) that usually causes discomfort.

phobia—An extreme or irrational fear.

psychiatrist—A medical doctor who specializes in the branch of medicine dealing with mental, emotional, or behavioral disorders.

psychologist—A person who studies the mind and human behavior.

self-esteem—The level of confidence and satisfaction a person feels about himself or herself.

social loneliness—Loneliness that results from not knowing anyone, and having no social group to belong to.

social phobia—Also known as social anxiety disorder; a fear of social situations that results in an inability to have any kind of dealings with other people.

solitude—The state of being alone.

stress—The body's reaction to an external force, situation, or change.

FURTHER READING

Crist, James J. *What to Do When You're Sad & Lonely: A Guide for Kids.* Minneapolis: Free Spirit Publishing, 2006.

Ford, Jean. *Surviving the Roller Coaster: A Teen's Guide to Coping with Moods.* Philadelphia: Mason Crest, 2005.

Gootman, Marilyn E., and Pamela Espeland. *When A Friend Dies: A Book For Teens About Grieving & Healing.* Minneapolis: Free Spirit Publishing, 2005.

INTERNET ADDRESSES

Children, Youth and Women's Health Service: Feeling Lonely

http://www.cyh.com/HealthTopics/HealthTopicDetailsKids.aspx?p=335&np=287&id=1800

KidsHealth: When It's Just You After School

www.kidshealth.org/kid/watch/house/homealone.html

National Institute of Mental Health: Depression

http://www.nimh.nih.gov/health/topics/depression/index.shtml

HOTLINE TELEPHONE NUMBERS

National Alcohol and Substance Abuse Information Center Hotline

1-800-784-6776

National Suicide Prevention Lifeline

1-800-273-TALK (1-800-273-8255)

CONTRIBUTORS

Author **Hal Marcovitz** lives in Pennsylvania, with his wife, Gail Snyder, who is a coauthor of this book, and their two daughters. He has written more than ninety books for young readers. His other titles in the Flip-It-Over Guides to Teen Emotions series are *A Guys' Guide to Anger* and *A Guys' Guide to Jealousy*.

Series advisor **Dr. Carroll Izard** is the Trustees Distinguished Professor of Psychology at the University of Delaware. His research and writing focuses on the development of emotion knowledge and emotion regulation and their contributions to social and emotional competence. He is author or editor of seventeen books (one of which won a national award) and more than one hundred articles in scientific journals. Dr. Izard is a fellow of both national psychological associations and the American Association for the Advancement of Science. He is the winner of the American Psychological Association's G. Stanley Hall Award and an international exchange fellowship from the National Academy of Sciences.

A Guys' Guide to Anger; A Girls' Guide to Anger
ISBN-13: 978-0-7660-2853-1   ISBN-10: 0-7660-2853-4

A Guys' Guide to Conflict; A Girls' Guide to Conflict
ISBN-13: 978-0-7660-2852-4   ISBN-10: 0-7660-2852-6

A Guys' Guide to Jealousy; A Girls' Guide to Jealousy
ISBN-13: 978-0-7660-2854-8   ISBN-10: 0-7660-2854-2

A Guys' Guide to Loneliness; A Girls' Guide to Loneliness
ISBN-13: 978-0-7660-2856-2   ISBN-10: 0-7660-2856-9

A Guys' Guide to Love; A Girls' Guide to Love
ISBN-13: 978-0-7660-2855-5   ISBN-10: 0-7660-2855-0

A Guys' Guide to Stress; A Girls' Guide to Stress
ISBN-13: 978-0-7660-2857-9   ISBN-10: 0-7660-2857-7

GIRLS!

STOP

Boring Guys' Stuff
From This Point On!

FLIP-iT-OVER
GUIDES TO TEEN EMOTIONS

A Girls' Guide to

Loneliness

Gail Snyder

E Enslow Publishers, Inc.
40 Industrial Road
Box 398
Berkeley Heights, NJ 07922
USA

http://www.enslow.com

Copyright © 2009 by Enslow Publishers, Inc.

All rights reserved.

No part of this book may be reproduced by any means without the written permission of the publisher.

. **Library of Congress Cataloging-in-Publication Data**

Marcovitz, Hal.
  A guys' guide to loneliness : a girls' guide to loneliness / Hal Marcovitz and Gail Snyder.
      p. cm. — (Flip-it-over guides to teen emotions)
  Includes bibliographical references and index.
  ISBN-13: 978-0-7660-2856-2 (alk. paper)
  ISBN-10: 0-7660-2856-9 (alk. paper)
  1. Loneliness—Juvenile literature. 2. Girls—Psychology—Juvenile literature. 3. Boys—Psychology—Juvenile literature. I. Snyder, Gail. II. Title.
  BF575.L7M32 2008
  155.42'424—dc22

                                    2008007666

Printed in the United States of America.

10 9 8 7 6 5 4 3 2 1

Produced by OTTN Publishing, Stockton, N.J.

To Our Readers: We have done our best to make sure all Internet Addresses in this book were active and appropriate when we went to press. However, the author and the publisher have no control over and assume no liability for the material available on those Internet sites or on other Web sites they may link to. Any comments or suggestions can be sent by e-mail to comments@enslow.com or to the address on the title page.

♻ Enslow Publishers, Inc., is committed to printing our books on recycled paper. The paper in every book contains 10% to 30% post-consumer waste (PCW). The cover board on the outside of each book contains 100% PCW. Our goal is to do our part to help young people and the environment too!

Photo Credits: © iStockphoto.com/pidjoe, 41; Used under license from Shutterstock, Inc., 1, 3, 4, 9, 11, 12, 15, 17, 20, 24, 25, 28, 31, 34, 36, 37, 38, 40, 44, 46, 49, 51, 53, 56, 57.

Cover Photo: Used under license from Shutterstock, Inc.

CONTENTS

What Is Loneliness?

Heather had moved during the summer, and it was her first week in a new school. She really missed Tara— her best friend from her old neighborhood. And she missed the group of friends she used to eat lunch with every day. Although she sat with a couple of girls at lunchtime, Heather didn't know them very well. She felt miserable and alone, although she tried not to show it.

It's hard to feel alone and disconnected from other people. Such feelings can occur anywhere. Even though Heather was surrounded by other students in a crowded lunchroom, she was experiencing the painful feelings of loneliness.

Feeling lonely. Everyone has experienced loneliness at one time or another. It comes in different forms. Loneliness

After her family moved, Heather had a hard time making friends at her new school. She felt most lonely at lunchtime.

You and Your Emotions

A part of everyone's personality, emotions are a powerful driving force in life. They are hard to define and understand. But what is known is that emotions—which include anger, fear, love, joy, jealousy, and hate—are a normal part of the human system. They are responses to situations and events that trigger bodily changes, motivating you to take some kind of action.

Some studies show that the brain relies more on emotions than on intellect in learning and in making decisions. Being able to identify and understand the emotions in yourself and in others can help you in your relationships with family, friends, and others throughout your life.

may be a mild feeling of boredom. Or it can be a vague sense of something missing. Sometimes, it can be a powerful feeling of emptiness—of feeling forgotten, unneeded, or ignored by the rest of the world. Feeling lonely is a normal healthy emotion, although it can often hurt a lot.

When feelings of loneliness are mild, they typically last only a little while. You might feel bored or sorry for yourself,

Loneliness can be a major source of stress—the mental or emotional strain that is the body's reaction to an external force, situation, or change. Being stressed out can affect your health. You may have less energy, have trouble concentrating, and have frequent stomachaches, headaches, and muscle tension.

Did You Know?

- One in five Americans is lonely.

- On average, lonely people have blood pressure readings that are thirty points higher than those of people who are not experiencing loneliness.

- High blood pressure can cause heart disease.[1]

for example, if you are not invited to a certain party. Or you may be feeling lonely because you're new in the neighborhood and haven't found a friend to talk to. But you may later find out the party wasn't much fun. Or you may start meeting new people. Then those feelings of loneliness will quickly vanish.

At other times, feelings of being disconnected may be strong. And they may go on for a long time. When a person experiences long-lasting feelings of isolation and loneliness, he or she is suffering from chronic loneliness. Long-lasting feelings of abandonment or rejection can lead to physical and emotional problems, including depression, anxiety, and resentment.

The need to connect. Everyone needs friends. In fact, psychologists have found that all human beings have a drive to be connected in social groups and to have close relationships. When these needs are not met, loneliness occurs. Researchers refer to two kinds of loneliness: social loneliness and emotional loneliness.

If you don't identify with or feel part of a group, you are dealing with social loneliness. This can happen if you have trouble making friends or are new to a neighborhood. You have no one to hang out with, go to the movies with, or regularly eat

lunch with. Without social contact, it is difficult to form or maintain any strong relationships.

Emotional loneliness occurs when you don't have any close relationships with other people. A girl feeling emotional loneliness may long for a best friend or someone to date. Or she may wish to be closer to her parents or to another family member. With emotional loneliness, a girl believes that no one is there for her to share hurts and feelings. She has nobody to talk to, and so she keeps a lot of feelings inside.

Feeling lonely or choosing to be alone. If you think no one really cares about you, it can hurt—a lot! That's why loneliness is known as a negative emotion. You feel bad about not having close friends or much social contact. When you feel lonely, you feel sad. You can experience other negative

Science Says....

All humans have a physiological need to connect or have contact with others. So says neurobiologist Mary Carlson of Harvard Medical School. She studied infants and toddlers living in overcrowded orphanages in the 1990s in Romania. The children there received no hugs, toys, or attention. Carlson concluded that the lack of touching and attention stunted the children. Because they were neglected, they did not develop normally. Many had physical, emotional, and social difficulties. The young children could not form normal relationships with other kids. They were also unresponsive or fearful of others.[2]

emotions, too, such as fear of the future or anger about being left out.

These negative feelings that accompany loneliness are very different from the feelings you can experience when you choose to be alone. When you have made a choice to be away from other people, you are seeking solitude. Solitude differs from loneliness because you are happy about the situation. You have chosen to take time to be by yourself in order to accomplish something positive. Without the distraction of other people, you can spend time doing what is important to you. You can think about your values and gain a better understanding of yourself.

Shyness and self-esteem. When you want to connect with others, however, your ability to form new relationships can be affected by your personality. If you are shy, for example, you typically feel apprehension or worry when meeting new people. As a result, you may feel lonely because you have a difficult time making friends.

Shyness, or discomfort in social situations, is common for many people. In fact, almost half the people in the United States describe themselves as shy.[3] Although the majority of them manage to hide their nervousness when in unfamiliar situations, they still feel shy.

The term *Self-esteem* refers to the way you feel and think about yourself. If your self-esteem is low, you are unhappy or annoyed (or a little mad) with yourself. You may often put yourself down. On the other hand, if you have high self-esteem, you like yourself for who you are.

The ability to make friends is hard for people with low self-esteem.

Shy people often have low self-esteem, which means they don't think very highly of themselves. They may keep an ideal image of what they should be in their head, even though they can't ever realistically achieve it.

For example, a girl with low self-esteem may be very self-critical, quick to refer to herself as worthless or stupid. She can have problems making friends because she doesn't think she's good enough to deserve a friend. Or she may think that others like her only because they want something she has. Because low self-esteem hinders her ability to form close friendships, she can suffer from emotional loneliness.

Changes in life. Shyness and low-self esteem aren't the only factors that can influence whether you might feel loneliness. Changes in your life can also bring about periods of time when you feel isolated and alone. This is especially true if

You May Feel Lonely...

. . . if you are shy and have a hard time making friends.

. . . when others don't seem to accept you.

. . . when you move to a new place (new school or town).

. . . with major family changes (parents' separation or divorce, remarriage, parent or sibling conflict).

. . . you don't have anyone to share thoughts and feelings with.

. . . if you have low self-esteem.

the change resulted in loss: the loss of a parent because of divorce, the loss of a friend because of a move, or the loss of a relationship because of a breakup. The death of a family member or friend can often lead to intense feelings of grief and loneliness.

Difficulties dealing with change can also occur within you. As a teen, you are in a time in life when a lot of physical and emotional changes are taking place. You are going through the changes of puberty, as your body matures. At the same time you may be facing and dealing with pressures to do well at school or to fit in with friends. The stress of change can leave you struggling with feelings of loneliness.

Learning to cope. The first thing to keep in mind is that feeling lonely is normal. Most teenagers go through it. You're not the only one out there who feels the way you do. Just because you feel lonely does not mean there is something wrong with you.

You can deal with feelings of loneliness by recognizing that difficult times are challenges you can overcome.

Whether you are feeling lonely because of a lack of friends or because of a sudden major change in your life, there are things you can do. This book includes information that can help you understand your feelings of loneliness. And it includes tips on what you can do to make things better, as well as ways to help others who also may be feeling the pangs of loneliness.

Afraid to Make Friends

When Debi and her friend Bethany went to summer camp, Debi was surprised to see how easily Bethany made new friends. Debi didn't know what to say to break the ice, while Bethany had no problem talking to kids she had never met before. Although Bethany encouraged her friend to come along with the group whenever they went swimming, Debi usually refused. She didn't think Bethany's new friends liked her. Whenever she could, she stayed in her cabin reading, listening to music on her MP3 player, and feeling sorry for herself.

Shy people can be very self-conscious. They often think negatively about themselves and worry about what others think of them. As Debi watched her friend gain acceptance with a new crowd, she had a lot of self-doubt.

Instead of feeling sorry for herself, Debi could have taken steps to open up to new people.

Her negative thoughts went something like this: "No one cares about me," "The other girls just don't get me," and "I'm different from them."

When Debi had first arrived in camp, she had spent a long time studying the bulletin board's list of events. "If I look like I'm busy reading the announcements," she thought to herself, "I won't have to talk to anyone." Avoiding people was Debi's method of coping with

How Shy Are You?

Give yourself one point for each statement you agree with.

1. The thought of meeting new people scares me.
2. When I meet someone new, I panic over what to say.
3. I feel more comfortable staying at home.
4. Most people don't like me.
5. I don't like to ask people for help.
6. I'm uncomfortable at parties unless I know most of the people there.
7. I don't like to speak in front of a group.
8. I find it hard to talk to strangers.
9. I'm afraid to speak up because I might say something that will embarrass me.
10. I wish I were more outgoing.

If your score is four or higher, your shyness may be keeping you from making friends. Take a look at the tips on pages 16–19 for some ideas on overcoming shyness.

her shyness. The girls around her started up conversations, asking each other where they were from. Debi didn't join in. She looked calm and uninterested on the outside. But on the inside, her heart was pounding and her stomach was churning.

Feeling shy. Everyone feels shy at one time or another. Feelings of uncertainty and nervousness can occur when you meet strangers or are facing new experiences. Many people find shyness makes it hard when they want to talk to someone they like but don't really know. However, this mild kind of shyness usually doesn't last. Within a few minutes of starting to talk,

they become comfortable in a conversation. But for the person who is extremely shy, the uncomfortable feelings don't disappear. The conversation remains painful from start to finish.

Extreme shyness. Extreme shyness can make you have a hard time making new friends, or just talking to people you don't know. The extremely shy girl may feel so confused and unable to think clearly that she freezes up in conversation. Because she is insecure about herself, she may also think that everyone is secretly criticizing her. As a result, she may keep quiet in social situations to avoid embarrassing herself. She may even avoid places where she could meet people she doesn't know very well.

In many cases the extremely shy girl appears uninterested in others. Her nervousness makes her come across as a snob— like someone who thinks so highly of herself that she doesn't want to have anything to do with those around her. In truth, she is so worried about how she appears to others, she just can't be herself.

Extreme shyness can make a person experience very real physical symptoms. These signs may include dizziness, sweating, clammy hands, blushing, and a sick-to-the-stomach sensation referred to as "having butterflies in the stomach."

These signs of shyness are a result of the fear reaction. This natural survival instinct kicks in whenever people feel unsafe. The body reacts by going into the fight-or-flight

In a study of relationships among sixth through tenth graders, the Public Health Agency of Canada reported that as many as 22 percent of girls said they found it "difficult" or "very difficult" to make new friends.[1]

When you are shy around people you don't know, you can experience symptoms of fear such as a pounding heart and tenseness.

mode: It physically prepares to fight against a perceived danger or run away from it. The heart pumps blood faster, and breathing rate increases. The rush of fear can also cause blushing, sweating, and a queasy stomach. People who are shy suffer from fears about how others see them.

Causes of shyness. You may have a shy personality because that is the way you are biologically. Some scientists believe that the trait of being shy is carried by a certain gene or by several genes. (Genes are the units of heredity that help determine a person's characteristics. They are passed along from parents to their child.) If your parents tend to be shy, you may have inherited a chance of being shy, too.

Another factor that might cause shyness is the way you were raised. If you watched your parents avoid social gatherings, you might feel comfortable doing the same thing, too. This is called learned behavior. If your family dealt with uncomfortable situations by avoiding them, you could have learned to be the same way, too.

Yet a third influence on whether you tend to be shy can be previous experiences. This is especially true if you have had difficulty with strangers in the past. If you have been bullied by others, you will most likely do your best to avoid being around strangers.

Overcoming shyness. If you think shyness is a problem for you, you can do something about it. If you know you are shy but are interested in making new friends, you can use some of the following strategies:

Try to make conversation with people you want to know better. Do your best to push yourself to connect with others. It may be easier to initiate a conversation, though, if you practice ahead of time what you're going to say. Make a mental list of

Body language is a nonverbal form of communication in which posture, eye movement, facial expressions, and hand gestures can be interpreted as revealing the emotions a person is feeling.

three topics you feel comfortable talking about. Pick one and try starting a conversation with someone you'd like to know better. Then when the situation seems right, speak up. Because you practiced, you'll have the right words to start.

As you talk, be aware of your body language. Body language refers to the gestures and movements that can show what you are thinking. For example, when nervous, many people look stiff and avoid meeting the other person's eyes. However, the message this kind of body language is sending can be that you are angry. Even if you are feeling nervous, try to consciously make yourself look relaxed. While you are speaking, look the other person in the eyes and smile.

Don't do all the talking. Pause and give the other person the opportunity to speak. And be sure to listen. Nod your head and include occasional short comments that

Try not to let your body language show you are uncomfortable when you talk to someone. Crossed arms can be a telltale sign of nervousness.

The Dangers of Distorted Thinking

Many experts believe that lonely people typically suffer from distorted thinking. Here are some examples to look out for. If you find you're using any of these negative kinds of thinking, do your best to make a change:

All-or-nothing thinking. Viewing situations, people, or self as entirely bad or entirely good. A girl whose crush doesn't know she exists may think, "No one is ever going to love me."

Projecting. Making false assumptions about what other people are thinking. A girl has a movie date with a guy, but the guy is late and hasn't called. The girl thinks, "I know he doesn't really like me."

Filtering. Ignoring the positive things and focusing on the negative. After receiving many compliments on her new haircut, a girl is told by one person that it makes her look weird. She filters out all compliments and thinks to herself, "I know my hair looks awful."

Blowing things out of proportion. Making a catastrophe over events that are of little importance. Not having a date for the dance becomes an awful calamity or flunking a test becomes "an absolute disaster."

show you're listening: "You're right," "uh huh," or "I know what you mean."

Do your best to ignore whatever negative comments may be in your head. That's distorted thinking and it doesn't help. Stay positive!

Push yourself to connect with others by joining activities at school that interest you. Perhaps you enjoy plays but don't have the nerve to get onstage. You might try joining the stage crew or work with props behind the scenes. If you like to sing, you might join a chorus. This will give you the opportunity to get to know other girls who like to sing, too.

Although it can be hard, your effort to connect with others will become easier with practice. The most important thing you can do is take action. If you are upset about having trouble making friends, you can do something about it.

More Tips for Overcoming Shyness

- Plan ahead what you're going to say or how you'll handle social situations. To feel more comfortable, practice how the conversation might go. One way to do this is to role-play (put yourself in the role of, or act out the thoughts of, another person).

- When in a new situation, don't focus on yourself so much. Put your energy into learning about others and not on what others might be thinking of you.

- If you're scared of what might happen, try to imagine the worst-case scenario and then ask yourself this question: Is it really that bad?

- Be patient . . . don't expect to overcome your shyness immediately. But do your best to keep working at it![2]

Feeling Isolated and Alone

"I was just joking," Mai said. "Don't be such a baby." But Jamie was hurt that the person she considered her best friend kept on teasing her, especially after being told to stop. She finally told Mai she never wanted to have anything to do with her again. After that, both girls ignored each other for a while. But soon Mai was telling the other girls to keep away from Jamie. No one would sit with her at lunch, work on projects with her, or answer her text messages.

When a friend stops being a friend, you can feel lost and lonely. This is especially true if the friend is someone you once trusted and shared your secrets with. But you can feel even worse if that person who claimed to be a friend turns into a bully. Sometimes, teens who want to fit in with a particular crowd will tolerate teasing by bullies. But when teasing becomes cruel and makes a person feel lonely and isolated, something is wrong.

Feeling isolated by bullies. A common form of bullying that girls use with each other is called relational aggression. It refers

Mai and Jamie had a falling out that left Jamie feeling sad and lonely.

to hurting the girl by destroying her relationships with others. Relational aggression typically involves name-calling, spreading rumors and gossip, ignoring the person, or criticizing her. Sometimes bullies harass with insults and threats that are text messaged on cell phones or that appear on Web sites.

The isolation and loneliness resulting from relational aggression can be extremely painful for the victims. They feel anger and frustration as they wonder what they did to deserve such treatment. Many victims of bullying feel ashamed of themselves, thinking there must be something wrong with them. As a result, their self-esteem plummets. Although such thinking is wrong, it is hard for the victims

What to Do If You Are Being Bullied

1. Unless you believe you may be physically harmed, confront your tormentor. Look the bully in the eye and tell her, firmly and clearly, to stop.

2. Then get away from the situation as quickly as possible.

3. Tell an adult what has happened immediately. If you are afraid to tell a teacher on your own, ask a friend to go with you.

4. Keep on speaking up until you get someone to listen. Explain what happened, who was involved, where it occurred, and what you have done.

5. Remember, bullying is not your fault—don't blame yourself for what has happened.[1]

Have You Been Bullied Online?

If you can answer yes to any of the following questions, then you have been the victim of cyberbullying:

- Have you had personal information about yourself posted online without your consent?

- Has a private conversation between you and friend ever been posted without your knowledge or permission?

- Have you had an embarrassing picture of yourself posted online without your knowledge or permission?

- Have you been entered into a Web site survey or contest without your consent?

- Has anyone pretended to be you online?[2]

of bullying to overcome such negative feelings. The pain and feelings of worthlessness caused by bullying can last a lifetime.

If you are being bullied, don't keep your feelings to yourself. The bullying is not likely to go away on its own. You need to be upfront with the person who is tormenting you. Confront the bully and ask her to stop, if you feel safe doing that. Do your best to keep your temper. Bullies like to get a reaction like anger or tears. If you stay calm, you may take the "fun" out of the bully's teasing, so she'll stop. However, if the bullying continues, or if you don't feel safe confronting her, you need to talk to an adult about what is going on.

If you are aware of another person being bullied, try to step in and stop it. Studies have shown that bullying takes a heavy

toll on the victims. Kids who feel rejected by their peers (fellow classmates and friends) often hold on for many years to those painful feelings of being isolated and alone.

Evaluating friendships. When a friend behaves in a way that upsets you, you need to let her know. If the behavior continues, she has crossed a line that shows she is not really a friend. Don't hang around people who make you feel bad about yourself. Recognize when friends are being false and drop them. End the relationship and work at making new friends.

Look to develop friendships with people who don't gossip and put others down. If they act that way with other people, you never know when one day they may decide to do the same to you. Choose friends who accept and like you for who you are. That way, you can be yourself when you are with them. A good friend should be someone you can trust. You can share confidences with that person and know they will be kept private.

When Friendships End

- Be open and honest about how you're feeling without being unnecessarily harsh.

- Avoid name-calling and shouting, even if you're feeling angry. Eventually, your emotions will simmer down, and you'll be glad you kept your cool.

- Deal with your emotions in a healthy way: Write down in a journal how you're feeling to get it all out.[3]

When making new friends, be yourself. Don't pretend you are interested in designer clothes just because the girls in the group you want to join say they are. If you don't care about designer stuff, you'll soon get bored when conversations focus on the subject. When you share interests and values with your friends, you have a better chance of finding people you enjoy spending time with.

Don't judge new people based on previous bad experiences. For example, just because the behavior of one girl at school bothers you doesn't mean that all the girls in her group will act the same way. Instead, try to see each person you meet with an open mind.

Helping others who are lonely. One day at school, you may notice the new person in class looks uncomfortable. Or you may see a sad-looking person sitting by herself

When making new friends, be sure to avoid the "gossipy" girls who talk about others behind their backs.

If you see someone who looks lonely, give the person a smile and go over to introduce yourself.

at a lunch table. Just as you can help people who are being targeted by bullies, you can also give a hand to people who are suffering from loneliness.

One way that you can tell if people are lonely is to look at their body language. Do they avoid looking other people in the eyes? Are they usually slumped over or slouching? Do they keep their legs and arms tightly crossed? These gestures and

> "What loneliness is more lonely than distrust?"
>
> -George Elliot

positions can be interpreted as telling people to stay away. Despite the defensive body language, these people may actually welcome your attempts to make contact. Even a simple gesture like a smile can help.

Or you can take your efforts a step further and try to strike up a conversation. Recognize that it could take you several attempts before you get a positive response. Initially, you may find that your attempt to talk doesn't work. This can be true particularly if the person you are reaching out to has already experienced a lot of rejection. For example, a girl who has been subjected to a lot of bullying and teasing in the past may consider herself an outcast. And she may think your efforts at kindness are just an effort to make fun of her. Even if your actions don't seem to work, keep trying anyway.

Science Says....

According to studies comparing them with peers, people who are lonely have trouble making conversation. They ask fewer questions, talk more about themselves, and flit from topic to topic. Their conversations are awkward and tend to end abruptly.[4] The experience typically ends with the lonely person feeling rejected. As a result, she has an even more anxious feeling when faced with the next new social situation.

Helping a Friend

Do you have a friend who's going through a difficult time?
Here are some tips for providing support.

- Let your friend know that you're there for her and that your goal is to help her however you can.

- Listen, listen, listen. Make sure your friend has your ear whenever she needs it.

- Don't judge; offer advice only when and if it is asked for.

- Be patient . . . don't expect your friend to bounce back and be herself right away.

- Do something special and unexpected for your friend![5]

Make an effort to help the person who is struggling with feelings of loneliness. If you see the new kid sitting by herself in the lunchroom, sit down and start a conversation. If you think your little brother is having problems at school, get him to stay at the table after dinner and ask him to share his troubles with you. Go out of your way to share your company with friends or relatives who may be in hospitals or nursing homes. You may find that by helping to ease the pain and loneliness of others, you will also be managing your own feelings of loneliness.

Dealing with Change

Although it has been several months since her parents' divorce, Syreeta still feels sad that she no longer lives with both her mother and father. She worries that her dad will remarry and start a new family. That would leave him little time for her. Sometimes, she wonders if she was somehow responsible for her parents' breakup. Syreeta wishes she could tell her mother how she feels, but the last time she tried, her mother got angry. She said she didn't want to hear another word about Syreeta's father.

More than one million kids experience a divorce in their families each year.[1] And approximately 20 million kids under age eighteen live with only one parent.[2] If your parents are divorced, then you already know that the breakup of your home life can leave you feeling stressed and depressed.

Separation and divorce. Teenagers like Syreeta who are trying to adjust to their parents' divorce can experience many negative emotions, ranging from loneliness to guilt to

When parents get divorced, the children can feel as though their family is falling apart. For many of them, the family changes caused by separation and divorce can lead to loneliness.

In 2004, 17 percent of all children in the United States lived in blended families.[3]

anger. In extreme cases, kids troubled by divorce may have trouble concentrating on schoolwork, begin experimenting with drugs or alcohol, and even run away from home.

Major family life changes can occur after a divorce is final. In cases where there is less household income, the family may have to move to a less expensive home. There may also be less money for entertainment, presents, and new clothes. These changes can be stressful and become a source of conflict between parents and kids.

Sometimes parents might begin dating and get remarried. Relationships will change with the addition of a new authority figure—a stepmother or stepfather. With the blending of stepbrothers, stepsisters, or half-siblings into a new family, life for the children of divorced parents can become more difficult. Rather than try to compete for the attention of the mother or father they live with, some kids find the easiest approach in dealing with so many changes is just to withdraw from everyone.

If you are part of a blended family, you probably have experienced some difficult moments. After all, the divorce and remarriage were events outside your control. But, whether you

A blended family is formed when adults who already have children marry. The stepbrothers, stepsisters, or half-siblings join together, becoming part of a new family.

like it or not, you still have to deal with the effect on your life. If you have not been able to talk to your parents about how you feel, it is likely you feel emotionally isolated from the adults who are responsible.

Moving. Another upsetting life change is being uprooted from your old neighborhood and having to move to a new place. The result can be social loneliness—you've lost all the familiar people you used to hang out with. And the change can also cause emotional loneliness—if you've left your very best friend behind and have only made a couple of casual acquaintances.

Do your best to stay positive. Even if you're not happy at your new home or school right away, give the new place some time. Meanwhile, go out of your way to talk to people in

Making Friends After a Move

- Start a conversation with a classmate by giving him or her a compliment. You might say something like "That was a good report you gave in class today," or "You played a great game yesterday."

- Ask new acquaintances to tell you about themselves.

- Share information about your old school or city, but don't overdo it. Say where you came from and what you liked to do there. However, don't go on and on about how much better your old school was or how much you miss your old friends.

- Ask about what's going on in your new school and community.

your classes, and make an effort to join in on school clubs, activities, or sports teams. Don't think back about the way things used to be. Instead, get involved with new people and activities and think about how much better you'll be feeling about your move in another month of two. Don't be unrealistic about how quickly friendships form, or you're likely to be disappointed unnecessarily and perhaps only reinforce your feelings of loneliness and shyness even more. Remember that the new people need some time to get used to you as well.

Coping with illness or death. You can feel intense emotional loneliness with other major family life events, especially the illness or death of a parent or family member. When you lose someone you love, it can cause a lot of pain. There is sadness and grief about losing someone important to you. And you can experience fear, wondering what the future will bring.

If a close family member dies, you must deal not only with your grief but also with the possibility of other changes in your life. For example, you may find that others will depend on you to assume new responsibilities,

The death of a family member or friend can cause deep feelings of loneliness.

Chronic Illness and Loneliness

A long-term illness in the family can put you in the position of having to balance the needs of others with your own needs. This kind of conflict within yourself can lead to feelings of guilt, anger, or sadness. If you don't have anyone to talk to about what's going on and what you're feeling, you can be overwhelmed by loneliness.

Many kids must learn to handle their own serious illnesses. According to one survey, more than 30 percent of kids ages ten through seventeen years old are dealing with one or more chronic conditions.[4] Kids suffering from respiratory allergies, asthma, hemophilia, diabetes, or cancer can often feel isolated and alone. Their friends may have a hard time understanding their symptoms and surgeries, and they may have physical limitations on the kinds of activities in which they can participate.

However, there are specific services and programs that provide information, counseling, and guidance for such teens. Some organizations also sponsor activities that bring together people dealing with the same chronic illness. Support groups provide ways for these teens to support each other emotionally and socially.

such as caring for siblings or taking on extra household chores. And you may be feeling overwhelmed if you have assumed more responsibility than you are comfortable with.

Your changed circumstances could make you feel alienated from your friends, who might not understand what you are going through or know what to say or do. Your relatives might have difficulty dealing with their grief as well. As a result, you

may be feeling like you have no one to turn to. Many kids prefer not to talk about a death in their immediate family—instead they try to maintain as normal a life as possible with their friends. Some grieve, but only when alone.

Grief is a normal and healthy reaction to loss. If you have lost a parent or someone else who is close to you, recognize that you will need time before the pain caused by his or her loss decreases. Psychologist Elisabeth Kübler-Ross observed the feelings of people facing death or experiencing the death of loved ones. In the 1960s, she developed a general model of Five Stages of Grief, shown below. It outlines the emotional reactions most people go through when dealing with

Five Stages of Grief

Psychologist Elisabeth Kübler-Ross described feelings of grief as occurring in five stages:

Denial: "This can't be happening."

Anger: "Why is this happening? Whose fault is it?"

Bargaining: "If I do _____, this will not have happened."

Depression: "I'm too sad to do anything."

Acceptance: "What has happened or will happen can't be changed. I'm at peace with it and ready to move on."

The amount of time a person might spend in each stage can differ. Your personality, the support you get from others, and the relationship with the person you're mourning for can affect your feelings.

When someone close to you passes away, it's okay to feel sad. It's part of the healing process, and it's important to get those feelings out.

the death of a loved one. Everyone responds differently and the order of these stages or length of time people need to come to terms with their loss can vary.

To deal with your grief, it might help to create something that can serve as a memorial to your loved one—make a

scrapbook of favorite photos, plant a memory garden or tree, or participate in a fundraiser in his or her memory. To lessen your feelings of sorrow and loneliness, you might also seek out a friend, family member, or other trusted person with whom you can share your memories.

Don't keep grief to yourself. If you are feeling sad and lonely, try to let other people in your life know what's going on. Find people who you can talk to—who will listen to you and be there for you. It may be that you have to take the initiative. Ask a teacher, a religious leader, an aunt, or some other family member if you could have a talk. Then let that person know you need his or her help. Little by little, share yourself and your story. Then listen to that person's thoughts and advice.

An effective way to begin to heal for many teens is by joining support groups with other people going through the same problems. Trained volunteers or health professionals typically lead group discussions. Within peer support groups, teens have the opportunity to talk with kids their own age about their feelings. At the same time, they share advice with others who have experienced the same hurt. By joining peer support groups, teens don't feel all alone in their grief. And they have the chance to come to terms with the death or illness that has brought about a change in their lives.

Grief and loneliness can also occur when a relationship breaks up. Pangs of loneliness can follow after a fight with your best friend or boyfriend. Perhaps

If changes in your life are making you feel overwhelmed, you need to tell someone.

Learning yoga or meditation can be a good way to center yourself in times of stress and sadness.

whatever caused the argument can't be resolved. Or maybe it was simply time for the relationship to come to an end. But when any kind of close relationship ends, your sense of grief and loss can be overwhelming. This is especially true if you want to get back together and the other person doesn't want to. If you were close enough to this person to be comfortable sharing your thoughts, feelings, and weaknesses, you can feel intense emotional loneliness when the relationship ends.

Dealing with broken relationships is similar to dealing with a death or serious illness. It is necessary to move through similar stages of grief—denial, anger, bargaining, and depression. As you learn to get past the feelings of

rejection, you will eventually be able to accept what has happened and move on.

Change happens. If the changes going on in your life have left you feeling lonely and upset, there are some things you can do. First of all, take care of your health. Don't skip meals, and try to eat a nutritious diet. Stay active by playing sports, learning yoga, riding your bike, or getting involved in some other activity that you enjoy. Lift your mood by seeking out friends or getting involved with new activities at school.

Reach out to someone to talk to. If you can't talk to your parents, try speaking with another adult relative, your school counselor, or a clergy member. If you think that talking with a psychologist or a family therapist would help, tell your parents. A medical professional could also help you get in touch with a support group whose members are dealing with similar issues.

Work It Out!

Physical exercise can make you feel better. It causes the body to release natural, mood-boosting brain chemicals—or neuro-transmitters—such as endorphin and serotonin.

Dangers of Loneliness

Feelings of loneliness can affect your health. You may be sleeping poorly, or feeling stressed out. You may have recently gained or lost a lot of weight. Perhaps you're having trouble concentrating in school or are feeling depressed. Loneliness has been linked to all of these health problems. It is also thought to play a role in alcohol and drug abuse, depression, and self-harm.

Sleep disturbances and stress. A person suffering from chronic loneliness sleeps less well than the average person. He or she will wake up more often at night and

have a harder time falling back asleep. As a result, the person suffering from loneliness doesn't get enough sleep. And studies have shown that people suffering from loneliness wake up with an increased level of stress hormones in their body.

Hormones are chemical substances that signal the cells of the body to take a specific action. One hormone

When you are dealing with loneliness and stress you can have many sleepless nights.

The Surveys Say...

A 2003 government survey asked high school students if in the past year they ever "felt so sad and hopeless almost every day for two weeks or more in a row that they stopped doing some usual activities." More than one out of three girls—or 36 percent—said yes.[1]

that is affected by stress is cortisol. In lonely people, the increase of cortisol results in an increase in blood pressure. Higher blood pressure means the heart has to work harder than usual. This can damage the blood vessels and heart, resulting in stroke and cardiovascular disease.

Eating disorders. With the onset of puberty, a girl's body changes. During this time, she may be unhappy with how she looks—and become obsessed with the desire to exercise or restrict food in order to keep herself thin. At the same time she may be dealing with stress because of academic or social pressures. As a result, some girls develop unhealthy dieting habits that can lead to eating disorders.

Eating disorders often occur when a girl is dealing with stress or loneliness and has a distorted image of her body and herself. There are three common eating disorders in the United States that a girl may struggle with. One of them, anorexia nervosa, is self-starvation. A second is bulimia nervosa, which is the eating of excessive amounts of food (binging), followed by eliminating the food by intentional vomiting (purging). Both disorders occur when the person believes (often incorrectly) that she weighs too much. A third kind of eating disorder is

binging, or compulsive eating that is not followed by purging. Large amounts of food are consumed within a short period of time. The girl eats not because of hunger but in an attempt to relieve feelings of stress and loneliness. The disorder causes her to put on weight, which contributes to unhappiness over her appearance. Binging is related not only to loneliness but also to poor self-esteem and depression.

If not treated, eating disorders can lead to serious, life-threatening medical problems. Binge eating can cause obesity, which occurs when a person has a body mass index (BMI) of 30 or greater. (BMI is calculated by dividing a person's weight in kilograms by height in meters squared.) Obesity-related health problems can also result due to the disorder.

Treatment of eating disorders usually involves education about healthy ways of dieting. It can also include professional support and therapy in which the person learns new social skills and ways to cope with anxiety and stress in healthy ways that don't involve food.

Problems with body image can lead to eating disorders.

Depression. The sad feelings of loneliness can also lead to

Signs of Depression

These symptoms usually occur every day over a period of at least two weeks:

Emotional Symptoms:

Prolonged sadness
Emptiness
Low self-esteem
Guilt
Thoughts of suicide
and death

Physical Symptoms:

Sleep disorders
Eating disorders
Headaches
Stomachaches

Behavioral Symptoms:

Isolating self from others
Acting out anger
Conflicts with friends, parents, or at school
Alcohol or drug abuse[3]

depression. A depressed mood can result from many situations. But events that can cause loneliness, such as the death of a friend, a breakup with a boyfriend, or some other kind of loss can bring on feelings of depression. This is especially true of

Science Says....

Pets help ease feelings of loneliness. The companionship and emotional bond that exists between an owner and pet can help a person deal with changes and losses in life. In addition, the act of stroking a dog or cat can help a person relax. Since loneliness can be a risk factor in people recovering from heart disease, the fact that pets help lessen loneliness improves the odds that the heart patient will recover. Studies have shown that petting an animal can slow a person's heart rate and lower blood pressure.[4]

teens with low self-esteem. Studies have shown that they are more at risk of becoming depressed when they have to deal with stressful situations.

When depression lasts for at least two weeks, it is considered clinical depression. This is a mental disorder in which feelings of sadness interfere with the person's ability to work, study, and interact with others. Clinical depression is a serious health problem that can affect a person's ability to function in everyday life.

Studies have shown a link between isolation, depression, and suicidal thoughts. In one study, it was shown that girls who were isolated from peers or who had troubled social relationships were at greater risk for suicidal thoughts than are girls with close relationships with peers.[5] Nearly 5,000 teenagers commit suicide each year in the United States, making it the third-leading cause of death among teenagers.[6]

Substance abuse. Many of the health problems that accompany loneliness lead to substance abuse. Intense feelings of shame and guilt that follow binge eating can lead to the abuse of alcohol and other drugs. The person suffering loneliness and depression may look to deaden the pain she's feeling inside the same way. Such attempts to "self medicate" do not provide any solutions. And alcohol and drugs can cause additional problems when used illegally.

Treatment. If you or a friend is dealing with health issues related to loneliness, you need to get help. These disorders can be treated, and it is important that the person affected receives professional care. There are several different kinds of antidepressant medications that are used in treating depression. Trained therapists or counselors may also work with patients to help them improve feelings about body image, change behavior, and handle relationships. This kind of professional treatment and education is known as psychotherapy. In young adults, a combination of medication and psychotherapy has proved effective.

Helping a Friend

The feelings of isolation and loneliness that accompany depression can make it hard for a person to know when or how to reach out for help. If you believe a friend or family member may be suicidal, tell an adult or call the suicide prevention hotline number listed on page 61.

But I Want to Be Alone!

Emily liked being by herself. She was a very private person. She spent hours each day in her room at home writing poetry. Many of her more than 1,700 poems focused on ideas like hope, being alone, nature—and even death. Today, Emily Dickinson, who lived during the 1800s, is known as one of most important American poets of her time.

Not everyone who is alone is lonely. The poet Emily Dickinson was famous for living a private life. She preferred being alone. She used her time alone to reflect on various aspects of life that became the subjects of her poems.

Did you ever see someone sitting by himself or herself at the movies or dining alone at a restaurant? If you gave it any thought, you might have felt sorry for the person. However, many people like being alone. In fact, they seek solitude. **When you choose to be alone.** Just because you want to be by yourself doesn't make you lonely. When being by yourself makes you feel sad, you are lonely. However,

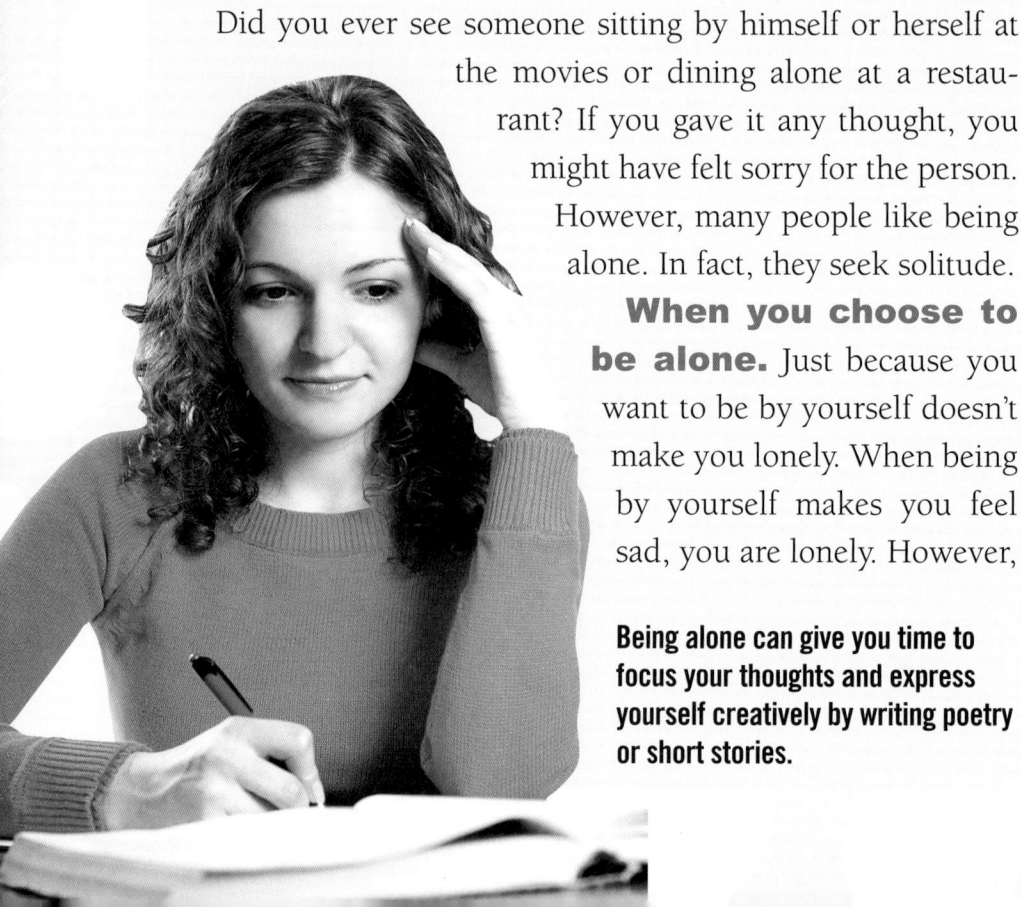

Being alone can give you time to focus your thoughts and express yourself creatively by writing poetry or short stories.

Are You Lonely or Just Alone?

1. There are lots of things I want to do when I am alone.
2. I'm alone because there is something wrong with me.
3. I like having free time to do what I want.
4. The best experiences in life are ones we share with other people.
5. I care about other people even when I'm by myself.
6. I'd rather do nothing than do things by myself.
7. By meeting my own needs I can do a better job of helping other people.
8. Most people only care about themselves.

If you agreed mostly with the odd-numbered statements, you probably enjoy solitary moments most of the time. If you agreed mostly with the even-numbered statements, you may be having issues with loneliness or low self-esteem.[1]

if you don't feel unhappy about being by yourself and long for something to be different, you are simply alone, enjoying solitude.

With solitude, you can give yourself the opportunity to connect with your inner thoughts and slow down the pace of your life. Solitude can provide a time for reflection. It can be a time for thinking and understanding yourself

"Loneliness is the poverty of self; solitude is the richness of self."

-May Sarton

and others. Or it may involve deep reading or simply resting at the end of a hike and enjoying the beauty of a sunset.

During quiet moments of solitude, you might find solutions to some of the problems that have been bothering you. You can be creative—perhaps writing a poem or song lyrics, or painting or sketching a landscape you remember or one that you imagine. You might make jewelry to give to one of your friends. Or you might want some time for yourself so you can listen to a CD from your favorite band, read a book, or write an entry in your journal.

Extroverts and introverts. Personality plays a part in how comfortable a person is with being alone. Some people are extremely outgoing—they are at their best when surrounded by others. Known as extroverts, such people have an easy time mixing with strangers. Although people with outgoing personalities may be okay with being alone from time to time, their overall preference is to be with others.

On the other hand, there are people who may be friendly and get along well with others, but their preference is to be

Spend your time alone relaxing and listening to your favorite tunes.

Myths About Solitude

Myth: People need to be with other people to be happy.

Fact: People can be content when they are by themselves.

Myth: Loners have poor people skills.

Fact: Many people who prefer to be alone are quite capable of interacting well with others.

by themselves. Known as introverts, they have more reserved personalities and are more private. They don't feel a strong need for other people's company.

Temperament will affect the amount of solitude a person needs. The extrovert tends to not need or want much alone time, while the introvert often prefers it. But regardless of their personality, all people can benefit from some periods of solitude.

Making the most out of solitude. When in solitude you can have the opportunity to learn more about yourself. It can be a time to reflect on questions like, Who are you? Where have you come from? Where are you are going? What are the most important things in your life? What do you want to accomplish? As you stop and think about who you are, you are gaining a better understanding of yourself. And as you are finding out who you really are, you are strengthening your own self-esteem, too. In this way it is possible for you to enjoy solitude—and benefit from experiencing it.

Overcoming Your Loneliness

Remember that you're not alone. Lots of people feel lonely at certain times in their lives. It's a normal feeling. But you can do something to feel better.

Evaluate what is causing loneliness. Try to put things in perspective. Think about what is causing you to feel lonely. Are you suffering from loneliness because of problems with making friends or a recent move, or both? Think about your behavior. Are your actions causing feelings of loneliness to get worse? That is, does your body language or apparently cold manner push people away? Instead of looking to friends and family for support, you may be straining your relationships because of your behavior. If so, recognize that it will be hard, but you are going to have to make changes in your behavior in order to connect with others.

If loneliness is a result of stressful changes in your life, such as a divorce or death in the family, don't keep your feelings inside. To make yourself feel better, you need to make an effort to share your thoughts with others. That will require reaching out and sharing yourself.

Reach out to others. Sitting at home feeling sorry for yourself won't accomplish any-thing. Realize that certain things in life

"Never be afraid to sit awhile and think."

–Lorraine Hansberry

Sometimes making a phone call can make all the difference.

will be tough. By learning how to deal with hard times, you will become a stronger person. Face the problem—no matter how much it hurts.

The key to defeating loneliness—at least for a time—is to take an active role in making your situation better. For example, if you miss your father who has been away for several weeks on a business trip, call him up. If you're feeling a bit down, invite your friend who usually makes you laugh to meet you for lunch. In other words, take the initiative to connect with someone else. (This works both ways, too. If you think a friend is feeling lonely, extend the invitation to her.)

If you don't get a response from the person you'd like to talk to, try again at another time. It may be that your dad was too busy to have time to talk when you called. You may need to catch him at a better time. If your friend can't make lunch because she has other commitments, ask if there is another time that she could meet you.

Tips for Dealing with Loneliness

- Stay healthy and elevate your mood by being physically active.

- Spend time alone working on a favorite hobby or try to learn a new one.

- Join new activities, such as after-school clubs, youth groups, or volunteer organizations, where you can meet new people.

- Share your hobbies and interests with others.

- Go out of your way to start a conversation with someone who is new to your school.

- Contribute to class discussions and conversations.

- Volunteer your time to a worthy cause.

- Spend time talking with family and friends, and limit time spent with television, books, and the Internet.

- If problems of loneliness persist, talk to a counselor or other trusted adult.

Even if you feel uncomfortable in social situations, avoid withdrawing. Instead, be the first to start a conversation. This can be true whether talking with family members, current friends, or complete strangers.

Work on making new friends. One way to do that is to talk to kids you have seen around before but never actually had a conversation with. You may feel awkward at first, especially if you feel self-conscious—like everyone is

Be open to meeting new people. You never know who may become your next best friend.

looking at you and judging you. In reality, they're probably not even aware. Think about it. How much do you really notice about what other people are doing?

Be open to people who are different from you. This doesn't mean that you should pretend to be someone you're not. Just try to be more open to learning more about other people. After all, your friends don't have to be exactly like you—dress like you do, do all the same things you like to do, and think like you do about everything. There may be some kids at school you've never thought of as possible friends because you have closed your eyes to them.

Does Loneliness Run in Your Family?

University of Chicago psychologist John Cacioppo believes genes play a part in how likely people are to experience loneliness. Cacioppo coauthored a study focusing on twins—both fraternal and identical. It included more than 8,000 young adults, ages thirteen to twenty years old. Participants were asked if they identified with statements such as "I feel lonely," "I like to be alone," and "Nobody loves me." Researchers found fewer differences in loneliness ratings reported by identical twins. The authors of the study believe that these results indicate loneliness may have a genetic component. That is, loneliness can run in families.[1]

In class, go out of your way to get to know new people. When the teacher tells students to form small groups to work on a special project, don't immediately join the group with people you know well. Instead, partner with the kids you don't know so well. The more times you try to connect with people you don't know well, the more chances you have to meet someone who could become a good friend.

Get to know people in the real world. Thanks to the Internet, there are ways to get connected with others without having to see them face-to-face. You can communicate through e-mail, chat rooms, and instant messaging. You can add your comments to blogs or visit someone's page at social networking Web sites.

However, recent studies have shown that when you do most of your communicating over the Internet, you don't practice the social skills that are important in face-to-face relationships. If

Social networking sites on the Internet can be a way for lonely people to meet others. However, studies indicate that time spent online takes away from time for family and friends in the real world.

you spend a lot of time on the Internet, you may initially feel less lonely. But studies show that teens who spend a lot of time online actually feel a deeper sense of loneliness. The online relationships they develop and maintain are a lot less meaningful than personal relationships they could be having with friends and family members. Some researchers warn that these teens don't learn how to socialize in the "real-world" because their experiences are only in the virtual one.[2]

Additional problems can arise with Internet use. Some people seek a solution to loneliness in online chat rooms or social networking sites, where they can meet up with strangers who

Does the Internet Make People Lonelier or Feel More Connected?

Some researchers have found that for every hour you spend on the Internet, the amount of time you spend interacting with members of your family drops by half.

Spending a lot of time online means you have less time to spend talking to your parents and getting to know your peers and other adults who affect your real life—such as your teachers, coaches, aunts, uncles, or grandparents.

Frequent users of the Internet who join discussion groups report that their interactions with strangers they meet online are less satisfying than face-to-face encounters.[3]

are not what they claim to be. For example, a forty-five-year-old man might say he is an eighteen-year-old guy in order to initiate a conversation with a teen. When using the Internet, keep in mind the tips for socializing safely online given on the next page.

Try a new activity or join a club. Look for your friends in the real world. At school, get more involved in activities. Sign up for a club that interests you. At the meetings, you may find some new friends who share your interests.

Or you might want to try doing something entirely new that's related to what interests you—for example, if you like working on science projects, you might like other things that involve hands-on work. Sign up for an art or shop class or

Internet Safety Tips

- Don't give out private information, especially passwords.

- Don't post information about yourself online that you don't want the whole world to know—and don't post other people's information, either.

- Don't exchange pictures with or give out e-mail addresses to people you meet on the Internet.

- Don't send a message when you are angry—it's hard to undo things that are said in anger.

- Recognize that online conversations can be copied, printed, and shared. They're not private.

- Use blocking features to keep people you don't want to talk to from bothering you during chat or instant messaging sessions.

- Be careful about making friends or flirting online. Because some people lie online about who they really are, you don't really know who you're dealing with.

- If you feel threatened by someone or uncomfortable because of something online, tell an adult you trust. Report your concerns to the police.

offer to help build sets for the school play. Or if the "thinking things through" aspect of the science project appeals to you, you might prefer to sign up for chess or math club, or to offer to be the play's backstage manager.

Get a part-time job or become a volunteer.
Get to know people outside of school. You might get a part-time job in an ice cream shop, restaurant, or grocery store—a place that employs other teens. You might want to look into volunteer opportunities such as helping out at an animal shelter or hospital. Visit with an older relative who may be feeling lonely. Not only will you feel good about helping other people, but you may also find new friends among your fellow volunteers.

Learn to feel better about yourself. If you believe that it's your own fault you feel sad and alone, you will find it hard to take any kind of action. Be positive about what you can bring to upcoming social events or activities— don't decide ahead of time that you will have a rotten time. To overcome feelings of loneliness, challenge yourself to think positively about who you are and what you've accomplished.

Volunteering at a tutoring center is a great way to meet new friends and sharpen academic skills at the same time.

Don't think of yourself as a lonely person. Accept the fact that like everyone else, you may be lonely now and then. However, don't let the emotion define who you are. Don't allow it to be an excuse for isolating yourself from others and withdrawing from life. Remember that making new friends takes time and does not happen overnight. Be patient, and be persistent.

Use your times alone to do things for yourself. When you are on your own, try to enjoy your solitude. Think of healthy or creative ways to spend

Turn feelings of loneliness into feelings of accomplishment by using time alone to develop new skills and abilities.

your time. Use the opportunity to read a book, work on a hobby, or play an instrument. Instead of sitting and watching TV, get active: Dance around to your favorite songs, go out for a bike ride, take a walk, paint a picture, or write poetry.

Don't wait for lonely feelings to go away. If they make you uncomfortable, do something about them! When you realize you're lonely, recognize that it is time to take action to bring about change in your life. Direct your focus and energy on reaching out to family. Work at making new friends. Stay positive, and you'll soon see that your efforts at overcoming loneliness will make a difference in your life.

Chapter 1. What Is Loneliness?

1. Robin Lloyd, "Loneliness Kills, Study Shows," *LiveScience*, March 31, 2006, <http://www.livescience.com/humanbiology/060331_loneliness.html> (April 15, 2008).

2. Mary "Maya" Carlson, "Developing Self and Emotion in Extreme Social Deprivation," *Project on the Decade of the Brain: Discovering Our Selves: The Science of Emotion*, January 3, 2000, <http://www.loc.gov/loc/brain/emotion/Carlson.html> (April 15, 2008).

3. Bernardo Carducci and Philip G. Zimbardo, "Are You Shy?" *Psychology Today*, November/December 1995, <http://psychologytoday.com/articles/pto-19951101-000030.html> (April 15, 2008).

Chapter 2. Afraid to Make Friends

1. "Chapter 4: Peer Relationships," *Public Health Agency of Canada*, September 2, 2002, <http://www.phac-aspc.gc.ca/dca-dea/publications/hbsc_04_e.html> (April 15, 2008).

2. Adapted from Jack Canfield, Mark Victor Hansen, and Deborah Reber, *Chicken Soup for the Teenage Soul: The Real Deal* (Deerfield Beach, Fla.: Health Communications, 2005), p. 24.

Chapter 3. Feeling Isolated and Alone

1. Adapted from Dorothea M. Ross, *Childhood Bullying and Teasing: What School Personnel, Other Professionals, and Parents Can Do* (Alexandria, Va.: American Counseling Association, 2003), p. 93.

2. Adapted from "Beware of the Cyber Bully," *i-Safe America*, n.d., <http://www.isafe.org/imgs/pdf/education/CyberBullying.pdf> (April 15, 2008).

3. Adapted from Canfield et al., p. 211.

4. Chris Segrin and Terry Kinney, "Social Skills Deficits Among the Socially Anxious: Rejection from Others and Loneliness," *Motivation and Emotion*, March 1995, pp. 1–24.

5. Adapted from Canfield et al., p. 227.

Chapter 4. Dealing with Change

1. Walter Kim, "Should You Stay Together for the Kids?" *Time*, September 25, 2000, p. 74.

2. Rose M. Kreider, "Living Arrangements of Children: 2004," *Current Population Reports*, February 2008, <http://www.census.gov/prod/2008pubs/p70-114.pdf> (March 12, 2008).

3. Ibid.

4. "Chronic Illness," *Mass General Hospital for Children*, 2008, <http://www.massgeneral.org/children/adolescenthealth/articles/aa_chronic_illness.aspx> (April 15, 2008).

Chapter 5. Dangers of Loneliness

1. "Youth Risk Behavior Surveillance System," *Centers for Disease Control and Prevention*, <http://apps.nccd.cdc.gov/yrbss> (April 15, 2008).

2. Kendra Lee, "What You Need to Know About Today's Teenage Girls," *Office of Minority Health Resource Center*, November/December 2000, <http://www.omhrc.gov/assets/pdf/checked/What%20You%20Need%20to%20Know%20About%20Today's%20Teenage%20Girls.pdf> (April 15, 2008).

3. "Young & the Lonely: A Team of Top Experts Answers Your Questions About Loneliness and Depression," *Science World*, February 7, 2003, p. 18.

4. Christine R. McLaughlin, "Furry Friends Can Aid Your Health," *DiscoveryHealth*, n.d., <http://health.discovery.com/centers/aging/powerofpets/powerofpets.html> (April 15, 2008).

5. David Williamson, "Research Reveals Social Isolation Boosts Teen Girls' Suicide Thoughts," *University of North Carolina News Services*, January 5, 2004, <http://www.unc.edu/news/archives/jan04/bear010504.html> (March 11, 2008).

6. "Suicide Facts at a Glance: Summer 2007," *Centers for Disease Control and Prevention*, n.d., <http://www.cdc.gov/ncipc/dvp/suicide/SuicideDataSheet.pdf> (April 15, 2008).

Chapter 6. But I *Want* to Be Alone!

1. Rae Andre, *Positive Solitude* (New York: Harper Collins, 1991), pp. 151–152.

Chapter 7. Overcoming Your Loneliness

1. "Loneliness Could Be in Your Genes," *BBC News*, November 11, 2005, <http://news.bbc.co.uk/2/hi/health/4426184.stm> (April 15, 2008).

2. Brent Staples, "What Adolescents Miss When We Let Them Grow Up in Cyberspace," *New York Times*, May 29, 2004, p. A-14.

3. Ibid.

anxiety—Feelings of fear, apprehension, and worry, usually over a future event.

binge—To eat large quantities of food.

body language—A subconscious form of communication involving body posture, facial expressions, movements, and gestures that often reveal what a person is really thinking or feeling.

depression—Extreme sadness; clinical depression is a mental disorder in which feelings of sadness, hopelessness, and loss of interest in life last for more than two weeks.

emotional loneliness—Loneliness resulting from not feeling close to or able to depend on another person.

endorphins—Mood boosting chemicals released by the brain during exercise.

extrovert—A person with an outgoing personality.

genes—The basic units of heredity that help determine a person's characteristics or traits.

hormone—A chemical substance that signals body cells to action.

introvert—A person who is quiet and has self-reliant qualities.

physiological—Having to do with the physiology, or biological functions and activities, of the body.

puberty—The developmental stage in which the human body matures to adulthood.

relational aggression—A nonphysical form of bullying in which a victim's ability to have relationships is damaged, usually by the spreading of false rumors and isolating the person.

self-esteem—The level of confidence and satisfaction a person feels about himself or herself.

social loneliness—Feelings of loneliness resulting from not being part of a group or having friends.

solitude—The state of being alone and without contact with other people, usually by choice.

stress—The body's reaction to an external force, situation, or change.

FURTHER READING

Clark, Travis, and Annie Belfield. *A Guys' Guide to Stress; A Girls' Guide to Stress.* Berkeley Heights, N.J.: Enslow Publishers, Inc., 2008.

Gootman, Marilyn E., and Pamela Espeland. *When A Friend Dies: A Book for Teens About Grieving & Healing.* Minneapolis: Free Spirit Publishing, 2005.

Silverstein, Alvin, et al. *The Eating Disorders Update: Understanding Anorexia, Bulimia, and Binge Eating.* Berkeley Heights, N.J.: Enslow Publishers, Inc., 2008.

Taylor, Julie. *The Girls' Guide to Friends: Straight Talk for Teens on Making Close Pals, Creating Lasting Ties, and Being an All-Around Great Friend.* New York: Three Rivers Press, 2002.

INTERNET ADDRESSES

Center for Young Women's Health: Dealing with Divorce and Separation: A Guide for Teens
http://www.youngwomenshealth.org/divorce.html

Girlshealth.gov: Relationships
http://www.girlshealth.gov/relationships/friendships.htm

Shykids.com: Teens
http://www.shykids.com/teensdirection.htm

HOTLINE TELEPHONE NUMBERS

National Alcohol and Substance Abuse Information Center Hotline
1-800-784-6776

National Suicide Prevention Lifeline
1-866-273-TALK (1-800-273-8255)

CONTRIBUTORS

Author Gail Snyder lives in Pennsylvania with her husband, Hal Marcovitz, who is coauthor of this book, and their two daughters. She has written more than ten books for young adults. Her other titles in the Flip-It-Over Guides to Teen Emotions series are *A Girls' Guide to Anger* and *A Girls' Guide to Jealousy*.

Series advisor Dr. Carroll Izard is the Trustees Distinguished Professor of Psychology at the University of Delaware. His research and writing focuses on the development of emotion knowledge and emotion regulation and their contributions to social and emotional competence. He is author or editor of seventeen books (one of which won a national award) and more than one hundred articles in scientific journals. Dr. Izard is a fellow of both national psychological associations and the American Association for the Advancement of Science. He is the winner of the American Psychological Association's G. Stanley Hall Award and an international exchange fellowship from the National Academy of Sciences.

A Guys' Guide to Anger; A Girls' Guide to Anger
ISBN-13: 978-0-7660-2853-1   ISBN-10: 0-7660-2853-4

A Guys' Guide to Conflict; A Girls' Guide to Conflict
ISBN-13: 978-0-7660-2852-4   ISBN-10: 0-7660-2852-6

A Guys' Guide to Jealousy; A Girls' Guide to Jealousy
ISBN-13: 978-0-7660-2854-8   ISBN-10: 0-7660-2854-2

A Guys' Guide to Loneliness; A Girls' Guide to Loneliness
ISBN-13: 978-0-7660-2856-2   ISBN-10: 0-7660-2856-9

A Guys' Guide to Love; A Girls' Guide to Love
ISBN-13: 978-0-7660-2855-5   ISBN-10: 0-7660-2855-0

A Guys' Guide to Stress; A Girls' Guide to Stress
ISBN-13: 978-0-7660-2857-9   ISBN-10: 0-7660-2857-7

GUYS!

KEEP OUT

Nothing But Girl Talk Ahead— You've Been Warned!